CHILDREN'S LIT.

ADLER

Get lost, little brother

DATE DUE			
AUG 20	¿		
DEC 12			
APR 06			

Get Lost, Little Brother

Other Clarion Books by C. S. Adler

The Evidence That Wasn't There
The Cat That Was Left Behind

Get Lost, Little Brother

C. S. ADLER

CLARION BOOKS

TICKNOR & FIELDS: A HOUGHTON MIFFLIN COMPANY

NEW YORK

Clarion Books
Ticknor & Fields, a Houghton Mifflin Company

Printed in the U.S.A.

Library of Congress Cataloging in Publication Data

Adler, C. S. (Carole S.)
Get lost, little brother.

Summary: When Todd and his brash friend
Louie decide to build a fort on the sandbar in
the river behind Todd's house, his older
brothers scoff at the idea.
[1. Brothers and sisters—Fiction]
I. Title.
PZ7.A26145Ge   1983   [Fic]   82-9579
ISBN 0-89919-154-1

V 10 9 8 7 6 5 4 3 2 1

FOR OUR SON KEN,
with love and admiration

Chapter 1

Todd sat on the lip of the blue bathtub, scowling at the bathroom door. He still couldn't believe his brothers would leave him locked in for the whole day. They had, though. He'd already heard the yellow school bus straining up the hill, stopping and starting again without him aboard.

Todd never missed school, never. How would he explain it to Mrs. Harris, his sixth grade teacher? "My brothers wedged the bathroom door shut and I couldn't get out." His classmates would find that hysterically funny. They'd look at him the way they had when the student teacher asked how many of them liked school and he, the new kid, was the only one who raised his hand. They were still treating him like an alien from another planet, although that had happened three months ago.

Todd stood up and kicked the bathroom door. Then he rammed his shoulder against it, only to be reminded by the sharp pain that he'd already failed to budge it twice before. Next he flopped stomach down on the cold white tiles and poked his fingers

1

through the narrow space under the door, trying to get a grip on the skinny end of the stuck wedge. It was rammed in so tightly it didn't even wiggle. No hope. When his brother Leon hammered something, it stayed hammered.

If only he'd unlocked the door and let his brothers share the bathroom with him when they'd demanded to be let in! He should have known better than to give them a hard time. Not only were there two of them, but they were two years older than he was. But Todd had a stubborn streak. Even when he knew he should give in, sometimes he couldn't make himself do it. After all, he was a person too. Besides, he liked his privacy in the bathroom. Also he hated being rushed, especially when he wasn't properly awake. "Just like your father!" his mother would say, and though she'd smile, Todd knew she didn't mean it as a compliment.

Most likely he'd be stuck in this bathroom until his brothers got home from eighth grade, he thought. They might not let him out even then. Suppose they made him wait until four, when his mother returned from her job as a speech therapist? He'd die from hunger. No, he wouldn't. He had read somewhere that a person can stay alive for months on just water. With all this plumbing around him, he could last for a year.

He groaned out loud, having just remembered that today his mother was going to a conference. She wouldn't be back until dinnertime, and Dad was, as usual, out of town. He was an engineer, working on a turbine project his company was doing in Saudi Arabia. *He* wouldn't be back until the weekend.

Todd climbed up on the toilet bowl lid and opened the window to survey escape prospects from there. He leaned out and looked down. Suicide. It was a twenty-foot drop, and even if he tied all the towels in the bathroom together to make a rope, it wouldn't be long enough. In front, their house was small and low to the ground, but back here, by the bathroom, the land fell away steeply down to the fringe of weeds and bushes at the marshy edge of the river.

Right about now he was supposed to be giving his oral report in social studies. It wasn't worth breaking a leg to get to school to give an oral report, but he felt bad about disappointing Mrs. Harris. He'd agreed to be first because nobody else was willing. Besides, he was eager to tell everybody why they shouldn't kill baby seals. All that stuff he'd read in magazine articles about how men went around clubbing helpless little animals to death — it was gross. Ladies could keep warm in fake furs just as well as in real ones. That was going to be his conclusion, to tell kids to go home and make their mothers give up fur coats. Did any ladies around here wear fur coats? Louie LaVoy's mother might. Louie's family lived in that house as big as a hotel across the road. People who lived in houses that big probably were rich enough to wear real furs.

Todd listened to the wind from the river scratching around the shutters. The mailman came around ten o'clock. Maybe Todd could attract his attention. The mailman would park on the road next to the barn-shaped boxes on posts, shove in the mail, and be on his way fast, without even needing to leave his truck. Todd would have to start yelling for help as soon as he heard the click of the metal latches opening, *if* he heard them from here at the back of the house. Then what? The mailman couldn't help anyway. He didn't have a key to the house. Useless.

Todd flipped through the stack of magazines on top of the toilet tank. Half were old *National Geographic*s he'd already read and the other half were his father's technical journals. Nobody besides Todd and his father liked to read in the bathroom, another habit they shared. Well, he'd rather be like Dad than like his brothers, who ran around hitting things all the time. They hit balls with bats. They hit punching bags. They even hit little brothers. They liked to kick too — doors and footballs and whatever part of Todd happened to be in their way. "Come on, turtle; move it, turtle," they'd yell at him.

This wasn't the first time his brothers had locked him up. When he was three, they'd locked him in a closet and told him vampires were going to get him. He'd screamed his head off in terror, but his mother was in the shower and didn't hear him. A stranger passing by had rushed into the house through an open window and rescued Todd.

He could yell all he wanted now. There weren't any nearby neighbors in this suburban town outside Schenectady, to which his family had moved in January. Their little brown house with the red shutters was stuck between two farms that nobody farmed anymore, one where an old man and his sister lived and the other owned by a young couple who were never home. Right across the road was a high wall of rock ledges.

The nearest house on the other side was distinguished by two things: It had an enormous weather vane with a mounted horseman on it and it was the home of Louanne LaVoy, the worst kid in school. She *would* have to be the only kid his age who lived near him. She was in his class too, but she spent most of her time in the principal's office getting detention. The principal shuddered whenever he saw Louie prancing down the hall toward him.

"Hi, Shatzy," she'd bellow. "You got me again tonight." She'd grin at him, and Mr. Shatz, who had mild brown eyes and a faraway look, would shudder. Todd sympathized with Mr. Shatz. If he had to sit with Louie every night and hear her crack her gum or yell out embarrassing comments, he'd shudder too. Louie's report was also going to be on seals. The student teacher they had now heard that they rode the same bus and assigned them the report to do together. The first thing Louie had said was, "Who wants to work with *him*?"

"I'm sure you'll make a good team," the student teacher had said. She probably said that because neither of them was too popular in class and Louie was a straight *D* student while Todd got *A*'s. She had a lot to learn, this student teacher. Todd couldn't imagine a worse matched team.

Just look how Louie had proceeded. First she'd checked out all the books on seals from both the school and public libraries before Todd got to them. Then, when he asked politely if she'd share her books with him, she said, "No way, professor. We're getting separate marks for what we hand in. Why should I give you a chance to get another *A* while I get a *D*? This time we fail together. Unless . . ."

"Unless what?" he had foolishly encouraged her, ignoring the fact that she'd tagged him "professor." It was just one of the nicknames kids stuck on him. "Professor" didn't even make sense because he didn't wear glasses and was as tall and sturdy-looking as his brothers, except a little narrower and paler.

"Unless you want to do my report for me," Louie said. "You could handle two reports easy enough from all the books I got."

"Can't you read?"

"Sure, but I've got my jogging to do and my TV programs to watch, and I got to do my workouts in the gym every afternoon."

"You work out in the gym?" He was puzzled.

"At home, stupid. My dad built a gym in our barn.

He lets me work out there. He thinks it's great I'm so tough." She flexed her arm muscles.

"I bet," Todd said.

"Anyway, if you want the books, you gotta do the work."

"No way," he said.

In answer she tossed back her long, brown, curly hair, which looked all wrong on her tall, boyish body, and marched off.

Todd had finally scrounged up a couple of articles from old natural history magazines his grandmother had given him. He also used *National Geographic*, which she'd subscribed to for him and his brothers before they even learned to read. His grandmother was a great believer in reading and in nature. Todd was too. And he liked math, especially computers. This morning at eleven he had time signed out on the terminal in the school library. Was it eleven yet? He'd wanted to try out the new game he'd designed. He wished he had the computer in the bathroom with him now. Then he'd be too interested to think about his empty stomach. It didn't look as if he was going to get any lunch unless he could find a way to escape.

He picked up his mother's magnifying mirror from the wicker shelf. If there were any boats on the river, he could signal an SOS with the mirror. Hanging out the window, Todd could see a stippling of white dots in the middle of the mud-colored water. Those were the gulls. He could hear their scree and caw, high and low. The world was a study in gray and tan and brown this early in April. A few ice chunks were still left under the trees at the river's edge. The trees on the far side of the river looked like gray bristles broken only by the white roof of a house that had a rotting boat dock extending into the water. There were no boats at all.

Todd had reread two *National Geographics* by the time his stomach told him it was noon. Then he took another look out the window. From the river right in back of his house came the *chk chk* of a bird standing on the tiptop twig of the skimpy tree on the island about twenty feet offshore. The *chk chk* switched to a whistle and then to a gravelly roll call. That bird was a regular orchestra.

The shoe-shaped island had nothing on it besides the tree and the bird and some straw-colored weeds, but it looked like a great place to pitch a tent. It would be fun to sleep out on an island like that. He could be alone and close to nature and not too far away from home if anything happened. Was the island near enough to be considered part of their property? Todd couldn't remember seeing any island on the map in the town office building, where he had gone with his father about the survey of their lot when they were buying this place last fall.

If it didn't belong to them, then who would own that chunk of land? Maybe he could claim it. Todd's Island. That sounded impressive. He wondered if his mother would let him claim an island. She'd probably want him to share it with his brothers. That would ruin it, all right. They'd take over and keep him off, or they'd pretend they were Indians and tie him to a stake and roast him to death until someone came along to rescue him.

"How come they hate me?" he'd asked his mother once.

"They don't hate you. They just like to tease."

"But why?"

"Because you're their little brother."

It didn't seem like a good enough excuse to him. Not for all the things they did to him. They tied his socks into knots to try and make him late for school. They soaked his sheets on cold winter nights and told their mother he'd wet his bed. And now that the three of them had to share the expanded attic bedroom upstairs, it was even worse.

"It's just like a big dormitory," their mother had said. She was trying to make them like this too-small house, which was half the size of the one they'd moved from in Ohio when Dad got transferred. They hadn't been able to sell their big house in Ohio yet, and until they did they couldn't afford to build onto this one.

At first Todd hadn't minded the idea of sharing the attic with his brothers. He sort of enjoyed eavesdropping on their conversations. But it hurt his feelings when Leon had protested to Mother, "You want us to sleep in the same room with *him*?"

"Why do we always get stuck with that baby?" Michael had said.

Todd didn't understand what they disliked about him. Sure he had his faults, but so did they. Why did they have to treat him like some kind of insect and go around trying to squash him all the time?

Todd suspected it was mainly the fault of that fifth grade math contest he'd won last year in Ohio. Leon really had it in for him because Todd's picture was in the papers and their parents had acted so proud about his winning a countywide contest. It wasn't Todd's fault. His teacher had made him take the test.

"You better not get any ideas, twerp. You're just a pain in the butt, even if you did win some contest," Leon had said.

From his spastic stomach Todd judged that lunch-time was long past. Still not a boat in sight. His nose began to drip from the chilly air, so he shut the window. Through the glass he could watch the clouds on their leisurely passage across the sky. He saw a blue jay chasing a wren and considered writing a list on the bathroom mirror of all the birds he could identify. He could write with his mother's mascara, but he needed his father's binoculars for proper bird identification.

He started memorizing an article on Australia's Great Barrier Reef. Knowing material like that by heart could come in handy if he ever had to make a speech. The bathtub turned out to be a pretty comfortable place to doze and daydream. Finally, when he had given up hope that the afternoon would ever end, he heard the front door slam. His brothers were five feet away in the kitchen.

The refrigerator door squeaked open. Should he begin to kick the door down now or play it cool and wait for them to let him out? The house had only this bathroom and the half one downstairs. Someone would need this one eventually. All of a sudden Todd couldn't wait another second. "You let me out of here now!" he bellowed.

They laughed. He could hear them. Leaving him here all day was their idea of a joke. He cursed them with the worst words he knew. Why had he gotten stuck with such rotten, mean brothers? "I'm going to tell Ma what you did to me," he yelled in desperation.

Silence. Then Leon's deep voice sounded right at the door. "You do and you're dead."

"Let me out then."

"You better promise you won't tell."

"I promise, I promise. Open the door."

"Swear it."

"I won't squeal on you, never. I won't say a word. Just let me out of here," Todd begged.

He heard them scrambling around. Then the wedge was hammered loose and the door opened.

"I hate you guys," Todd said into the grinning faces of his twin brothers. "You make me puke." Then he stalked out of the bathroom with all the dignity he could muster.

11

Chapter 2

Todd opened one sleepy eye and saw sunlight on the rag rug in the center of the bedroom floor. He was tempted to slide back into his dream — it was an interesting one about landing on an asteroid large enough to explore. But something alerted him to danger.

Sure enough, when he opened both eyes he saw that Leon's bed was empty. Todd sat up. Michael was out of the room too. Would there be another bathroom lockout or lockup this morning? Not too likely. His brothers prided themselves on their inventiveness; they wouldn't repeat the same torture. Besides, it would be risky to keep him out of school a second day. The school called home if you didn't show up for two days in a row.

Todd checked to make sure his seal report was still safe under his mattress. It was. He'd retrieve it just before leaving for the bus. Ever since he'd had to pay his brothers a whole week's allowance to get back a book report of his they'd hidden, he'd taken precautions.

Reluctantly, he picked up the note Leon had forged last night to explain Todd's absence from school. Leon had said Todd stayed home because of a stomachache, and signed their mother's name. It grieved Todd to use it, but he didn't see what choice he had.

He dressed quickly and scooted downstairs. His mother was dishing out a specialty of hers, fried eggs cooked inside holes cut in bread. "I was just going to send Michael up to wake you, Todd," his mother said. "Want an egg in a nest?"

"Uh huh," he said. "Good morning, Mom." He went to use the bathroom, careful to leave the door ajar so he wouldn't get locked in. By the time he was through, his mother had his breakfast on the table and Leon and Michael had already left for their bus.

"So how's school going, Todd?" His mother stood sipping her coffee in her stockinged feet. She always put her high heels on at the last possible minute.

"Okay. Good, I guess."

"Still no friends, though, huh?"

"I told you, Mom, none of the kids in school live around here." Louie was too weird to count as a kid.

"I feel so bad that we stuck you in a place where there's no one your age."

"Well, don't worry. I'm okay alone."

"Of course, you've got your brothers."

"Yeah." Todd sighed deeply.

"What's wrong, darling?" Her milk chocolate eyes shone on him with concern. He used to think she could read his mind when she looked at him like that. She was a pretty lady with melting eyes and round, soft cheeks. He knew she really loved him a lot, and he loved her back as much. It wasn't her fault about his brothers. She'd had them first and was stuck with them.

"Everything's fine, Mom. I'm going to turn in my seal report today."

"I thought it was due yesterday."

"I'm handing it in today."

She didn't question him. She rinsed out her coffee cup and stepped into her heels, getting ready to deal with all the lispers and stutterers in her care.

Todd only had to cross the road to get to the school-bus stop, which was right beside the rank of four mailboxes. His family's box said Lewis. Louie's box said LaVoy. He saw her come flying down her long curved driveway at the same time that the blunt yellow nose of the school bus showed around the curve.

"Well, well, well," she said, skidding to a stop in front of him so that she could get on the bus first. "So you decided to show your face today, eh, professor?"

"Move it, Louie. You're holding up the line," Todd said even though it was just a two-person line. She hoisted herself into the bus and slid into the first seat up front. Todd looked desperately for an empty seat. The only one was next to Louie. She patted it, grinning at him as if she dared him to take it.

"Siddown," the driver snarled at Todd. He was a bulldog-faced man who appeared to hate kids. Cursing his luck silently, Todd sat next to Louie.

"That's why you stayed home yesterday, isn't it, professor?" Louie said "Because you didn't have your report."

"No."

"Why'd you stay home then? You sick?"

He looked at her warily. Her question sounded innocent enough, and she looked like a sweet little girl today in a candy-striped dress. The hiking boots she wore only spoiled the effect a little. "My brothers locked me in the bathroom," Todd admitted.

"No kidding. For the whole day?"

"The whole day."

"Why'd they do it?"

"Just for fun."

She laughed. "No kidding! Bet your brothers aren't as tough as my brother, though. Mine lives in Arizona now because Dad kicked him out when he got in trouble with the law."

"Oh, yeah? Do you miss him?"

"Not so much . . . a little sometimes. He never paid any attention to me."

"My brothers aren't that bad," Todd said. "They're nice to me sometimes."

"Yeah? Like when?"

15

Todd thought. While he was thinking, the bus traversed the whole of River Road and made the turn up the street to their elementary school. "They buy me birthday presents," Todd said at last.

Louie snorted. "Big deal! Your mother makes them do that."

"They let me use their stuff — sometimes."

Louie yawned as if the subject was beginning to bore her. Todd brooded. His brothers were not bad kids. They made friends easily. People liked them, more people than liked him. He wondered uneasily if something was wrong with him. He couldn't think what, though. His mother liked him, and as far as he could tell he was a pretty decent person, compared to other people. At least, he didn't lie or steal or deliberately hurt people's feelings.

Just before they turned into the school grounds, Todd asked Louie, "How'd you do on your report yesterday?"

"Oh, okay," she said. "I copied it straight from the books."

"That's cheating."

"So what? I've done it before and nobody caught me. You got to be smart enough to leave out the big words and shorten up the sentences, that's all."

"But even if you don't get caught," Todd said, "it's still cheating."

"So?"

"So that stinks. Besides, you don't have to cheat. You're not dumb."

16

"My dad says anything you can get away with in this world is okay. He says it's all a game anyway."

"You're not supposed to cheat at games either," Todd said. "What is your father, some kind of crook?"

"No," Louie said. She didn't even sound a little insulted, although Todd knew he would have been if anyone had said that to him. "My dad manages houses. He collects rents and he owns part of a tennis club."

"But there's got to be some kind of rules," Todd said, "and not cheating's one of them."

"*You* play by the rules," Louie said. "Just see how far it gets you."

The bus driver pulled up to the back bumper of the last school bus in line at the curb and released the door so that it folded back. Louie climbed over the railing between the front door and her seat to be first off the bus.

The bus driver exploded. "Get back in here, you!" he yelled. He hauled her back in and made her exit again, "like a lady."

Todd had to laugh with the rest of the kids as Louie minced off the bus on the tiptoes of her hiking boots and turned to drop a curtsy to the bus driver. She was a devil all right, not afraid of anybody, Todd thought with admiration.

The day went well for Todd. His unit test in math came back with 100 percent written large across the top in bright red. Miss Lowry, the student teacher, complimented him on the collage he'd done for his seal report cover. It showed a seal cut out of fake fur pasted on a picture of arctic landscape with some wildlife conservation stamps and a headline about saving baby seals from slaughter. "Was this your own idea," Miss Lowry asked, "or did your mother help you?"

Todd got red and was about to defend his honor when Louie piped up, "Todd's a genius, Lowry, don't you know?"

"I'm not a genius," Todd protested. What had he ever done to make Louie brand him with such a damaging label? Professor was bad enough. Genius would keep him from ever making friends. Louie grinned back at him.

Later, when Miss Lowry was busy in another corner of the class, Louie said, "Don't worry, kid. I know you only got ordinary smarts — like me."

"Go bug somebody else, huh?" he said.

After lunch Todd gained a whole hour on the computer terminal in the library because of a mix-up in the art teacher's schedule. The game he'd invented worked perfectly. Besides that, Mrs. Aceto, the librarian, handed him the biography of Buckminster Fuller he'd ordered, called *Pilot for Spaceship Earth*. He'd have something good to read tonight when his brothers settled down to watch people shooting and chasing one another on TV. All in all, he counted it a good day. Until he got home.

Todd stuck his key in the front door lock and

turned. Nothing happened. The lock seemed to open, but the door didn't. He tried again and shoved with the shoulder that was still sore from yesterday. No luck. He walked around the foundation planting and down the hill to the back of the house. The garage was closed, but the back door next to the garage door should work. It didn't. He peered through the nearest window and could just make out the edge of his father's workbench. It had been shoved up against the back door. Todd wondered what his brothers had used to blockade the front door — the couch maybe. They had repeated themselves after all, but this time they had locked him out instead of in. He was hungry and he wanted to use the toilet. Could they have forgotten to lock the windows in the laundry room?

He dashed around the house to see. Locked. He looked up because he thought he heard laughter, and got a water balloon dropped — splat! — on his chest. It wet the whole front of his windbreaker, which wasn't waterproof. The wind was blowing and it was pretty chilly out. Did they want him to get pneumonia and die?

"Hey, you guys!" he yelled. "This time I'm gonna tell if you don't let me in."

A round, freckled face with mischievous blue eyes and prickly hair appeared at the window to grin down on him. Leon. Leon was built like a bull, broad and strong. Adults thought he looked cute. Michael was blond, brown-eyed and tall, a dreamer.

He was the handsome one. The twins didn't look at all alike. They weren't much alike either. Leon was a heavy-duty engine and Michael was more like a steering wheel.

On his own, Michael was agreeable and easy to get along with, but he followed his twin brother's lead in everything, including bugging Todd. Sure enough, Michael's face appeared behind Leon's shoulder in the window. There was no way to fight back at two of them. And if Todd told on them, what good would it do him? Mom specialized in easy punishments that didn't fit the crime. "No dessert," was her favorite, or "no television," or "no allowance." That didn't take the fun out of bugging little brothers, not nearly.

Todd turned his back on the house and marched down the naked, yellow-green lawn to the riverbank. He had to think up a good way to get back at them. In the meantime, there was no point in giving them the satisfaction of seeing his frustration. He pulled his jacket off and hung it on a tree. Then he put the tree trunk between himself and the house. Let them think he was drowning himself.

He relieved his full bladder in the weeds, which were just brown stems in the rock-strewn mud at the river's edge. Right in front of him was the island he'd noticed from the bathroom window yesterday. Up close it looked bigger, more like a woodchuck than a shoe. The broad part was flat and wide enough for a tent, all right. It would be great to have a camp of his own. There he could relax and not have to guard himself or his belongings against attack all the time. In front of the tent he'd build a firepit lined with rocks, so he could stare into the flames of a campfire and warm himself on a dark night.

He wondered how deep the channel was between his yard and the island. Could he wade across? Probably not, and the water was too polluted for swimming even if it were summer. They did have that rowboat Dad had bought in Ohio and never used much. It would be a cinch to get across to the island in the rowboat. What about using it alone, though? It was likely to be another one of those things his parents would only let him do with his brothers along. That just showed how little parents understood. Todd would be a lot safer doing things without them.

"You going swimming?" a voice called.

He turned to see Louie hiking down the patchy grass of the hill toward him, bold as if she'd been invited.

"It's too cold for swimming," Todd said.

"Not if you're a polar bear."

"Do I look like a polar bear?"

Without answering, Louie squatted on the damp ground beside him and looked out at the river. She was chewing gum, cracking it loudly as usual. She drove teachers crazy by suddenly cracking her gum in the middle of a lecture. Todd wondered if she chewed the same piece every day. He wasn't going to give her the satisfaction of asking, though. She loved telling him he was stupid.

"What are *you* here for?" he asked ungraciously.

"Came to see what you were doing."

"Nothing."

"Same as me. So what are you looking at? There's no boats on the river this early."

"I'm thinking of building a camp on that island," he admitted.

"Is it yours?"

"Well, I don't know. It could be part of our property, and if it's not, and nobody owns it, maybe I can claim it."

"Hey, like the explorers. That's neat," she enthused. "You gonna plant a flag and make a speech and everything?"

"I could." She had made it sound romantic. Todd's Island! I claim thee in the name of myself, Todd Lewis, he thought, smiling to himself. Then he'd post No Trespassing signs that said: Leon and Michael — This Means You!

"Want me to help you make a flag?" Louie asked.

"Well, I don't know," he stalled.

"I've got a ski pole we could use and plenty of rags. What color do you want?" she asked. "Green, red, blue?"

"I don't know. I'll think about it." She was rushing him out of dream and into reality. He hated being rushed. Besides, he didn't need help from her. "Louie, I'll make my own flag if I decide to have one."

"Sure, it's your island." She snapped her gum. "Want some?" She offered him an open pack of gum sticks. So, she used fresh, he noted.

"Thanks," he said and took a piece.

"Take two," she said. "One's never enough."

Two sticks of gum! She was a generous kid. "After I get the flag made, you can help me with the flag-planting ceremony, if I have one," he offered. After all, he owed her something for the idea.

"Sure. That'd be fun. We could do it on a sunny afternoon after school and get the newspapers to come and take a picture of us. We could have a party and sell drinks and cookies. I could do posters to tell all the kids in school about it. I'm pretty good in art."

Todd's jaw sprung open. She was whipping plans past him faster than cars speeding under a highway bridge. He could see his private, peaceful spot turning into a public free-for-all before his very eyes.

"Hold it," he said. "I'm not sure I want anybody to even know about this place. If my brothers get wind of it I'm dead. That flag would just be target practice for them."

"How can you hide a camp that's right under their noses?" She looked back at the house and he followed her gaze. Two heads were clearly visible in the kitchen window. "They're watching us right now, aren't they?" she asked.

"Yeah," Todd said with a sinking in his gut. He was going to be in for some heavy teasing tonight. Talking to a girl! They might even think he'd invited her here. They'd get a year's worth of embarrassing cracks out of that. He'd have to explain that Louie might have hair like a girl's, but otherwise she qualified as a boy, a pretty tough one too. Hadn't Todd seen her knock the wind out of the biggest kid in sixth grade? That had been on Todd's first day at school here. She packed some wallop, Louie did.

"I like a challenge," Louie said, eyeing the heads in the window. "It makes things more interesting."

"Listen, Louie, I don't think —"

"Let's shake on our partnership." She held out her hand. Automatically, he reached out and they shook. She had a grip as hard as Leon's.

"I'm with you all the way, professor," she said. "We're really going to make something out of this deal."

He winced. What had he just done? He and this tough guy-girl were now partners. Impossible! Worse than that, a disaster in the making. He needed time to think. The sight of his mother's red compact swinging into the garage gave him an excuse.

"I've gotta run," he said. When he looked back over his shoulder, Louie was grinning at him. She waved and took off for home.

Chapter 3

"Hi, honey. How're you doing?" Todd's mother greeted him as she reached up to swing the garage door down. Despite her cheerfulness, her face looked smudged with tiredness. She liked her job, Todd knew, but it did wear her out. He appreciated that she managed to keep a supply of love and understanding just for him, no matter what. At least where mothers were concerned, he was lucky.

"I'm okay," he said and then followed through on his threat to tell. "But Leon and Michael locked me out of the house this afternoon."

"They did? How could they?"

"They blocked the front and back door with furniture."

"Those boys are such teases!"

It would be just a "no dessert for dinner" punishment. Todd could hear in her voice that she didn't take locking him out too seriously. To make it worse, the evidence had disappeared. The workbench was back under the fluorescent light where it belonged, and no doubt the couch would be in place upstairs, if it was the couch they had used.

"Todd says you locked him out of the house," Mother said to the twins, who were sprawled on the floor in front of the television.

"He's crazy," Leon said. "The little baby don't know how to use his key, that's all."

"Doesn't," his mother said.

"Yeah," Leon answered. "Can I have a piece of whatever you got in that bakery box, Mom?"

"No, these are tarts for our dessert tonight. We'll eat them *after* dinner." She set the box down on the kitchen counter and noticed the mess of banana peels, spilled juice, peanut butter with a knife sticking out of the open jar, and bread crumbs. She groaned. "Can't you kids clean up after yourselves when you snack? Leon, you and Michael clean up this kitchen right now."

"Why us?" Leon demanded. "Why don't you make Todd clean up too? Boy, he sure gets away with murder around here."

"Basket!" Michael yelled, tossing an empty soda can into the open plastic garbage pail.

"Todd doesn't have to clean up a mess he didn't make," Mother said. "Why did you lock him out of the house anyway?"

"You always take his part," Leon said. "We didn't lock the baby out."

"You *did*," Todd put in.

"Prove it," Leon said.

"I can't. You got rid of the evidence."

"You see, Mom?" Leon flashed his eyes sincerely at her. "He's always trying to get us in trouble."

"Lying is bad for your mental health, Leon," Mom said dryly.

"I'm not lying."

"He is," Todd said.

"Michael, did you and your brother lock Todd out or not?" Mother asked.

"Aw, Mom, it isn't even cold outside," Michael said.

"But you guys lied!" Todd yelled.

They all began shouting at one another. Their mother put her hands over her ears and said breathlessly, "Listen, kids, I am very, very tired tonight. Do you think you could manage to get along with one another without a referee for just one evening? Please!"

It made Todd angry that his brothers didn't even get deprived of their dessert. Nothing happened to them. They could probably kill him and get away with it. Dad would back up Mother as usual, or else he'd punish everybody for what he called "disturbing the peace." It was useless to expect help from his parents.

Todd retreated to the living room to brood about how to get back at his brothers. When Michael came to tell him it was his turn to set the table, Todd snapped, "I'm busy. You do it." He could short sheet his brothers' beds or empty a tray of ice cubes into them, but those were baby tricks. He needed to think of something worse. If only he was better at thinking up mean things to do! His stomach knotted with frustration.

To soothe himself, Todd picked up one of the photograph albums on the lower shelf of the bookcase. The albums recorded so many peaceful and funny moments of his life. Besides, it encouraged him to see how far he'd come from babyhood. There he was in his mother's arms, helpless, googling at the camera, and there he was nose to nose with a neighbor's dog at two, and there playing with a toy dump truck under a Christmas tree at four.

He was half his brothers' size in a picture of the three of them when he was six, up to Leon's shoulder in a lineup on a ferry boat when he was nine. But this evening, as Todd studied the familiar record of his growth and development, he noticed something that had never struck him before. Immediately he flipped back to the beginning of the album and began a rough count. There were six pages of Leon and Michael before he ever appeared. That was normal. He hadn't been born yet. But after he was born, he estimated, there were three times as many pictures of Leon and Michael alone as of him. A chill went through him. It was just like the baby books. Mother had a full one for Leon and Michael, but she claimed to have lost his. Did his *parents* hate him too?

Todd waited until after dinner when Michael and

Leon left him alone with Mother to do the dishes. Then he asked, "Mom, how come there's so few pictures of me in the photograph album?"

"What do you mean, Todd? There are as many of you as of your brothers."

"No, there's not. I counted. There's three times as many of them. How come?"

"I don't know, darling. Your father probably just got tired of taking baby pictures."

"*You* could have taken some of me."

"I'm no good with a camera. You know that, Todd."

"What's he complaining about now?" Leon asked, coming into the kitchen for an after-dinner snack. Leon's hunger pangs struck hourly as long as he was awake, but no matter how much food he consumed, he never gained weight.

"Todd's just making an observation, not complaining," Mother said. She gave the bottom of the pot one last scrub with the steel wool, rinsed the pot and handed it to Todd to dry.

"See, you're defending him again, Ma," Leon said. "Babies get away with everything in this house."

"No, they don't," Todd said. "They get dumped on all the time in this house."

"Oh, so you admit you're a baby," Leon said. He accidentally stepped on Todd's foot as he reached past him to get a clean glass. Todd promptly kicked him in the shins. Leon cuffed him and Todd went wild. He threw himself at Leon and tried to pound him, but Leon pinned his arms and Todd ended with his head banging against the refrigerator.

"Basket," Michael said, as he arched a Cracker Jack box across the kitchen at, but not in, the garbage can.

"All of you stop fighting this minute or you march straight up to bed!" Mother yelled. The edge of hysteria in her voice was a blinking yellow light signaling caution. They all quieted down fast. Leon released Todd, who took one last swing at him and missed when Leon ducked.

"Turkey," Leon said and the fight was over.

"I can't go to bed; I got to write a composition on drugs," Michael said. "It's due tomorrow."

"Drugs?" Mother asked anxiously. "Why drugs?"

"Because that's the only topic that looked good."

"Oh," she said. "Well, what do you know about it?"

"Not much."

"I think I have some pamphlets that I saved from a conference. Let me see if I can find them." She handed Todd the last pan to dry and went to the desk in the living room.

Mother was always eager to be helpful if it had something to do with school, especially for Michael who spent as little time as possible on schoolwork and was satisfied with just getting by. Leon liked to get high marks. It made him angry when he didn't, even though he never put in the extra time that high marks cost. Leon acted as if he ought to be rewarded with an A for just being Leon.

Todd watched his mother sifting through material for Michael. It was hard to tell with Mother who her favorite was, if she had a favorite. She gave her attention to whoever needed it and spread love around to whoever would accept it. As for Dad, if he favored any of them, it was Leon. At least Leon was the one Dad always put in charge. Todd wondered if his parents loved Leon and Michael three times as much as him or was the lack of pictures of him really just a mistake?

He thought of the island. It would be comforting to have his own special place. Tomorrow, first thing, he'd get down to the town offices and see if anybody owned that land. Then if nobody did, he'd claim it. He'd better ask for permission to use the rowboat, though. The island was no use unless he could get to it.

Tomorrow night his father would be home. Todd estimated his chances of getting his father's permission as less than fifty-fifty. Dad was a pessimist. He always thought of bad things that could happen. Mom was a better bet to say yes. She liked to give them what they asked for unless it was harmful or expensive.

Patiently, Todd waited until his mother had finished helping Michael get started on his composition. "Don't you have a paper to do too, Leon?" she asked.

"No, I finished mine in school."

"What's it on?"

"Football."

"Oh, Leon, not another one on football!"

"Sure, Mom. I got a lot to say on the subject. Don't worry. I'll do good."

"That's not the point. The point is are you learning anything?" Mother asked.

"Nobody learns anything from old Tippytoes," Leon said. "He's just waiting to retire. . . . Is it okay if I stay up late tonight? There's a good movie on TV."

Ten minutes of argument followed about whether the movie was worth staying up late for, whether a horror movie merited watching at all, why Leon couldn't read a good book instead of rotting his brains out with TV, how staying up late once a week wasn't going to kill him (that was Leon's side), and how ten o'clock bedtimes were ridiculous for kids his age (that was Leon's side too). As usual, Mother let him have his way.

She finally retreated to the far corner of the couch, curled her feet up under her, and opened the novel she was reading. Todd sneaked quietly onto the couch next to her. She reached an arm out and hugged him absently. He let her hug, then pulled back before Leon caught them at it. Leon only let Mom kiss him once a year, on his birthday. "Mom," Todd began softly. "Could I just ask you one thing?"

32

"What's that, Todd darling?"

"You know that rowboat Dad's got in the garage?"

"Yes, I know it well. Every time I drive into the garage, I expect it to crash down on the hood of my car."

"Yeah, well, the ice is out of the river now. We could launch it."

"Believe me, I'm going to encourage your dad to get it out of the garage."

"This weekend?"

"If he's not too busy. What's with the rowboat, Todd? Thinking of taking up fishing?" She mussed his hair, which was wavy like Michael's.

"No, but I need the rowboat for transportation," Todd said.

"Transportation to where? Todd, you can't go out alone in the river in that thing, you know. The current's too strong."

"Don't worry. I only want to pole over to the little island that's just off the bank a few feet. I wouldn't go anywhere else."

"What island?" Michael asked. He was standing on the stairs with his notebook in hand. Todd hadn't even heard him coming down because Leon had the television on so loud.

"Todd's interested in that little sandbar in front of our property," Mom said.

"That thing? There's nothing on it."

"Nothing much," Todd said.

"So what do you want to row over to it for?"

"Just to explore."

Michael came the rest of the way down and handed Mother his notebook, asking her to check over his punctuation and spelling. "I'll row with you if Dad won't let you go alone," Michael said to Todd.

Too bad Michael wasn't his only brother, Todd thought. They could get along fine, but Michael's first loyalty was to his twin, and no way could Todd get along with Leon. Todd hoped Michael wouldn't mention the island to Leon, but he didn't dare risk asking Michael not to say anything.

During the commercial break in the horror movie, Leon lunged across the small living room and tackled Michael. He fell onto the rug, but rolled out from under Leon and got to his feet. Then Michael surged back at Leon, who waited for him in a wrestler's crouch.

"Not in my living room," Mom cried. "Stop that, you two. Be careful of the coffee table. Leon, you may *not* watch the rest of that program!"

"Ah, it's no good anyway," Leon said. He butted his head into Michael's midsection.

Todd watched the wrestling match with mild interest. Michael was bigger, but Leon was better at pushing and shoving and ramming people. Leon could end up as a professional football player someday. Neither of their parents would be too pleased if he did. They admired people who used their brains well, not their muscles, but Leon had brains too and he sure had energy to burn.

"I'm warning you," Mother tried again. "Stop it or there'll be serious consequences." Leon and Michael ignored her. They'd have stopped immediately if Dad were home.

"Oh, why didn't I have girls!" Mother moaned. "Being an only child never prepared me for this."

Leon pinned Michael. "I got you," Leon announced.

"Yeah, you got me," Michael agreed.

Leon stood up satisfied. He had won. "So what's this about exploring an island?" Leon asked.

Todd gulped. His project was doomed. Leon had heard.

"You know what we could do," Leon said, "is make a rope bridge over to the island. Remember that TV show we saw? It'd be fun to swing over on a rope bridge."

"Absolutely not," Mother said. "No rope bridges over water. Suppose one of you fell in?"

"We can all swim, Ma," Leon pointed out.

"Oh, no!" Mother said, "I hope I'm not going to regret picking this house because it was right on the river!"

"Relax. Relax. Take it easy," Leon said. "You worry too much, you know?"

"When your father gets home, you can discuss the island with him, but *no* rope bridges," Mother said.

Already Todd's island had become a family project. Not to mention that Louie LaVoy was involved too. He couldn't believe how fast he had lost control. No doubt, in a day or two his brothers would forbid him to step foot on *their* island. Well, not this time. Not if he could help it. He might be the baby brother, but he'd show them he could fight back. As for Louie, he had to think what to do about that problem too.

Chapter 4

"You come over to my house after school for a strategy meeting," Louie said to Todd.

She had just been delivered to their classroom door by an enormous hulk of a man wearing a jogging suit. He told Mrs. Harris in a Papa Bear voice, "Sorry she's late. The bus left before we finished our run this morning."

"That's quite all right, Mr. LaVoy," the teacher said. "I'm sure running with her father is good for Louanne."

Mr. LaVoy nodded in agreement. Instead of leaving, however, he peered from under a hedge of black eyebrows at the other members of his daughter's class, as if checking to see how they measured up to her. "Yeah," Mr. LaVoy said to nobody in particular, "she's in good shape for a kid."

Mrs. Harris riffled the attendance cards impatiently while a polite smile curved all the many lines of her face upward.

"Yeah," Louie's father said. He nodded to himself and abruptly departed.

Everyone who had been watching this performance now resumed their low-voiced chatter, and Mrs. Harris got down to the business of checking off the absentees.

"Okay?" Louie asked and nudged Todd with her elbow to get his attention.

"Go to your house? I guess so," Todd said. He was curious to see the inside of that huge establishment anyway.

Since it was a Friday, Leon and Michael had a ball game after school. Todd had the house to himself. That suited him, but the invitation to visit Louie interested him more. He hiked across the road and up Louie's long driveway. Her house sprawled out in all directions, with three separate wings attached and several outbuildings behind it. Todd was staring up at the mounted horseman weather vane on the steep roof when Louie opened the front door before he'd even rung the bell.

"Want a milkshake? I'm having one," Louie said.

"Well, sure, if it's not too much trouble." Todd had been so eager to come that he'd left home without getting a snack first.

Laughter sputtered from Louie as she led the way into the anteroom where the glorious sweeping banister for the main staircase curved around two walls.

"What's so funny?" Todd asked.

"You," she said. "You're so polite; you sound like a girl."

"Girls don't have a monopoly on politeness," Todd said severely. He wasn't going to let Louie walk all over him. It was bad enough to have older brothers doing that. No kid his own age better try it. "You'd get in a whole lot less trouble if *you* were polite," he added.

"I know that," Louie said. "And you'd have a lot more friends if you weren't such a stiff."

"Listen, Louie," Todd said. "I don't need insults from you. I'll see you in school." He turned on his heel.

"Hey, don't go. I'm sorry," she said and grabbed his arm. "Come on, don't be mad at me. I promise I'll keep my big mouth shut."

He considered. She had a firm grip on his arm and she did look sorry. "Okay," he said and let her lead him through a dark hallway to an enormous high-ceilinged kitchen. One whole wall was brick and hung with shiny copper pots and molds. An indoor barbecue was built right in. The rest of the kitchen had more fancy appliances than Todd had ever seen in a Sears Roebuck catalog.

"Boy," Todd said. "You must be rich, Louie."

Louie shrugged. "Nah. My mother says we're just well off."

"I'll say."

"The best thing we got is the gym. My father put in one of those Universal fitness machines. He lets me work out on it too. And we got a hot tub. I'll show you after we drink our milkshakes."

"How many brothers and sisters do you have?"

"Just the brother I told you about, the one that took off."

"Three people in this big house? You must have more than a room each for yourselves."

"Yeah, so what?"

"So, you're lucky," he said and concentrated on enjoying the thick and creamy chocolate milkshake.

"Listen," Louie said. "I been thinking about the island. Did you check out how we're going to get there? Because I got a neat idea. We could build a rope bridge over to it and —"

"My mom already said no to that. My father gets home tonight and I'll ask him about using the rowboat. I have one problem, though."

"What's that?" she asked.

"My brothers found out."

"So?"

"So, anything we set up out there, they'll tear down."

"Unless —" she said and paused dramatically.

"Unless what?" He hated being left in suspense.

"Unless — Did you ever hear the expression 'The way to beat them is to join them'? We could ask your brothers to join us."

"No way. They'd take over. It would be *their* island. They'd make the rules and I'd end up locked out."

Louie considered. At rest her face looked sweet.

She even looked sort of pretty, except for the milk mustache. She sucked up the last of her milkshake noisily, alerting Todd to the fact that he'd only gotten a third of the way down on his. He concentrated on drinking. He was always the last one in his family to finish eating.

"I guess the first thing to do is be sure it's legally yours," Louie said.

"Right. I'm going down to the town offices to see about that as soon as I can."

"And then," Louie continued, "we should build something out there, like a fort."

"A fort?" Todd said. "All we need's a tent and a firepit so we can camp."

"I thought you just said your brothers would wreck anything you put there. We need something we can defend, like a fort."

"What're we going to build a fort out of?"

"Railroad ties," she said.

"Too heavy, and where're we going to get them anyway?" Todd asked.

"We just happen to have a big pile of them out back. Dad was going to build a retaining wall for the garden, but then he decided to build a drywall out of stone instead."

"But Louie, you and I can't carry railroad ties. Those things weigh a ton. They're loaded with creosote."

"So we'll get a lot of kids to help us."

"Why should anyone want to help us?" Todd

asked. "You figuring on paying them or something?"

"No. We'll just tell them if they want to join our club, they've got to help build the fort."

"What club?" he asked in alarm. Here she went again, turning his private camp public right under his nose.

"Our club. Todd's Island Club. You can be president."

"I don't want to be president."

"Then I'll be president," she said too quickly. "I always wanted to be president of something but nobody'd ever elect me."

"Listen, Louie. I don't want a club. This is a private island — *my* island."

"Sure, sure. Todd's Island, that's what we'll call it. But how are you going to keep it after you claim it? Anything you build on it, your brothers will take over. Right?"

"Right," he said reluctantly. She was backing him into a corner faster than he could think of a way to escape.

"So if you've got a club," she said with convincing logic, "you could put guards on duty at the fort. You could have an alarm system so we could run out and defend it. We could sling mudballs at anybody trying to scale our walls. We could dump pails of water on —"

"I want a peaceful island, not a war." Todd stood up. She was definitely not the partner for him.

"Listen," Louie said. "It's not *me* making the war; it's your brothers."

Todd wavered, then sat down again slowly. She was right.

"Come on," Louie said. "I'll show you the railroad ties and the gym. Then we can go up to my room and make the flag. Unless you already made it. Did you?"

Todd shook his head. He hadn't gotten around to it. He followed her across a flagstone patio toward what had once been a barn. From the back, Louie looked as long-legged and narrow-hipped as a boy, and she had a stride like a boy, too. Maybe his brothers hadn't teased him about her yet because they hadn't noticed she was a girl despite the long curls bouncing on her shoulders.

The railroad ties were impressive, a huge pile of six-foot lengths all nicely weathered so that they would not be sticky to lean against. "We could put posts in the ground," Todd said, thinking out loud, "and stack the ties up against them. They'd stay up if we tilted the posts in a little toward the middle. But what'd we use for a roof?"

"Oh, we've got plenty of stuff," Louie said. "There's a whole shed full of parts of old buildings. Including a chicken coop roof in good condition."

"And your father will let us use all this?"

"Oh, sure, he won't care."

Todd was so busy mulling over construction details that he paid little attention to the gym, of which

Louie was so proud. She demonstrated the body building machine while she babbled about pectorals and deltoids and biceps, but he barely heard her. He was thinking the rowboat would carry one or two railroad ties over at a time and maybe even the chicken coop roof. But what about dragging those heavy railroad ties from her house across to his? That was going to be a problem. Then, did they need doors and windows? They could always leave one end of the fort open and hang a sheet of plastic over the opening to keep out the rain.

It might be kind of fun to have a club so long as they kept the membership down to just a few kids. The island certainly wasn't big enough to accommodate more than three or four kids at a time. Who would they ask? He was still thinking about that when Louie ushered him up the back stairs to her bedroom. From the closet she dug out a box with enough material to make flags for a fleet of yachts.

"My mother thought I'd get interested in sewing," Louie said to explain the box.

"Can you sew?" Todd asked.

"Not even a button."

"I can. My mother taught us all how. Leon's the best. He sews patches on all his jeans."

"No kidding? Your brother *Leon* sews?"

Todd nodded. "He's good with his hands. He can build anything." That was another reason their father liked Leon.

"Well, pick what you want," Louie said. Todd

44

selected a red and white checkered fabric that had once been a tablecloth.

"What are you going to say on it?" Louie asked. "Todd's Island Club?"

"I don't know yet," Todd said.

"Well, hurry up and decide. We want to have a flag-raising right away, don't we?"

"Not necessarily. Flags are easy to rip down. We'd be better off getting the fort built first and then running up the flag."

"You got a point," she said. "We'll get our club started and get the place built and then call up the newspaper and invite them to our flag-raising ceremony. I bet they'd be glad to put our pictures in the paper."

"Louie, hold it. What do we need to advertise for? Let's take one step at a time, huh?" Todd appreciated her enthusiasm, but her speed made him nervous.

"We need some kind of important purpose for our fort," Louie mused, as if he hadn't spoken. "It's got to be kind of like — We could say it's for kids to hide in when they're in trouble at home or with the law. Freedom Island or —"

"No!" Todd said firmly. "It's not an outlaw camp."

"What're we going to use it for, then?" she asked, turning sullen.

"Like a nature preserve. Someplace to relax and be quiet."

"Rats," Louie said. "Who wants to sit around with a bunch of bugs?"

"Okay, if you don't like it, forget it. It's my island." He still had the tent his parents had given him last Christmas. In a pinch, he could use that.

"Oh, don't get huffy," she said. "You don't care if I get up a flyer, do you?"

"For what?"

"To tell kids about joining our club. I won't tell them I'm the president, though, or that it's your island."

"Why not?"

"Because then nobody'd join."

He knew neither of them was likely to be voted most popular kid in their class, but it hurt to hear he was a negative draw. Still, he had to admit she might be right. "Anyway," he said hopefully, "there aren't any other kids besides us around here, are there?"

"There's a whole street full right on the other side of this hill," Louie said. "I play basketball over there sometimes. How about we tell them to come around two o'clock on Sunday afternoon?"

"You mean this weekend, the day after tomorrow?"

"Why not?"

"It's too soon."

He hadn't even settled with his parents about the rowboat yet, and for all he knew, the island was somebody else's private property.

The sound of crunching gravel outside distracted Louie. She looked out the window and said quickly, "Listen, Sunday's plenty of time to do everything. Don't worry about it. . . . If you want to escape saying hello to my mother for an hour, you better leave now. That's her coming home from her bridge club."

Todd checked his watch. "I'd better go. My mother will be home too and Dad's due any minute."

"So, I'll see you." Louie leaned over the banister as Todd ran down the grand staircase. He was out the front door before Louie's mother finished parking her car in the garage.

Todd knew Louie's estimate of the hour it would take to greet her mother was correct. Back in February, Louie's mother had kept Mrs. Harris talking long past their allotted conference time and upset the whole parent-child-teacher conference schedule. Todd's mother had been annoyed because she had just started her new job and had to get back to work. But when Todd repeated what he'd heard Louie tell Mrs. Harris, that Louie's mother belonged to five bridge clubs, one for each day of the week, his mother surprised him by saying, "Poor woman. She must be bored out of her mind."

It seemed strange to Todd that his mother should feel sorry for a lady who spent her time playing games instead of working. Time-wasting struck him as an enjoyable luxury.

His family was already seated around the thick maple table when Todd ducked into the kitchen. His father was listening to Leon and Michael describe their ball game.

"Hi, Dad," Todd said. "Did you have a good trip?"

"So-so," Dad said. He always said "so-so," even if it had been a success. He was a solid, serious-looking man who did a lot more looking and listening than talking. The way Todd saw it, his father did the judging and made the laws in the family while his mother was the chief executive, just like the branches of the government. Having a female president was all right with Todd. He'd lived with one all his life.

"How come you're late, Todd? It's past six," his father said.

"I was at a friend's house and I lost track of the time," Todd said. "I'm sorry, Dad."

"So long as you don't make it a habit." Dad smiled at Todd briefly and took another bite of his grapefruit.

"Hey, Dad," Leon said, "Todd wants to get the rowboat out of the garage tomorrow so we can use it on the river. Can we? It's supposed to be in the sixties and sunny tomorrow."

"If I have time," their father said. "I have a long list of things that have to be done first, and I've got to go down to the plant for a few hours to look through the mail and fill out my expense account."

48

"I'm sure the boys can wait, Warren," Mother said. "Don't push yourself."

"But if you can, Dad," Leon said, "it won't take us five minutes."

"We'll see," Dad said. He would never promise anything, but he always tried.

While he chewed his pork chop, which was on the dry side, Todd puzzled over why Leon had brought up the subject of the rowboat. Was he really doing Todd a favor? It seemed unlikely. It could be Leon was planning to claim the island for himself.

Todd thought of the checkered cloth he'd left at Louie's house. If he didn't get a move on, the island would be snatched away from him. Tomorrow he'd better get down to the town office building somehow and check out that survey map.

Chapter 5

Todd lay in bed trying to bring the day into focus. Even though it was Saturday, he had awakened with a sense of urgency. He struggled to untangle himself from the dreams of the night — something to do with curling up in a dark burrow for safety. Guppies were in it too, swimming past his eyes. His prettiest guppy mother had had her babies last night, and he'd stayed up late seeing to it they were secure.

He rolled out of bed and went to check the tank. It was perking along nicely, thermostat working, air bubbling. The babies were swimming pinheads in the fry crib Todd had improvised out of wire and nylon mesh. Now what was it he had to do today? The island — the town offices — the rowboat. Oh, yeah.

"Mom says if you want any pancakes you'd better get downstairs fast," Michael said from the doorway.

"I'm coming."

Michael was wearing his baseball cap. He and

Leon had a game this morning. Todd made a sudden connection. The town offices were right behind the ball field. He already had found out they were open Saturday mornings. He could hitch a ride with whoever drove his brothers to the game. Good. That solved one problem.

"Leon, how could you take the last of that syrup?" Mother was asking when Todd entered the kitchen. "Now there isn't any left for Todd."

"He can use jelly," Leon said.

"How can you be so selfish?" Mother asked.

"Maybe it'll teach Todd to get up on time," Dad said, and to his youngest son, "Good morning, slugabed."

"Good morning," Todd mumbled. He spread butter and brown sugar on his pancakes and pretended he liked them that way.

"Dad, you gonna watch us play this morning?" Leon asked. "You said you would last time, remember?"

Their father put down the agricultural supplies ad he was studying from the Saturday paper and looked at Leon. "I'm sorry, son. I told you I was short on time this weekend."

"But Dad, all the other kids' fathers watch. Last week I pitched a no-hitter."

"Good," Dad said dryly. "Someday you'll be a pro ball player and make a fortune, no doubt, but meanwhile I've got a job to do if we want to eat."

"Mom works too," Leon mumbled.

"Her job has different demands. Mine is time-consuming. I'm not any fonder of the traveling I'm required to do than you are, but we'll just have to live with it," Dad said. Then his lip quirked up and he added, "I'm sorry about the ball game, Leon."

"Ah, you don't care about baseball anyway. You don't care about nothing I do," Leon said. His eyes flashed and his face was red. He had to be upset to talk back to their father that way.

"Leon," Mom said. "What's the matter with you? How can you feel sorry for yourself when you know you're luckier than ninety percent of the kids in this world? You've got a decent family, a roof over your head, plenty to eat, and a good future to look forward to. What do you want from your father?"

"Nothing," Leon said. "Just that he watch us play."

"Okay, enough of this," Dad said. "I'm going to the plant. I'll try to get home in time to repair that part of the front lawn that the truck tore up."

"Can you drop Leon and Michael off at the ball field on your way to work?" Mother asked. "I could pick them up on my way back from food shopping."

"Agreed," Dad said. He circled a lawn fertilizer on sale with a felt-tipped marker.

"Can I go too?" Todd asked casually. "To the ball field."

"How come you want to go to a baseball game?" Leon wanted to know. "You said baseball was boring."

"I don't have anything better to do this morning."

"You want to watch us play?" Leon asked.

"Sort of," Todd said.

"Yeah?" Leon sounded as if he didn't believe it, but when he got up to take his dishes to the dishwasher, he gave Todd a brotherly whack on the back. It was the kind of whack he often gave Michael, a Leon love tap. Todd was startled, pleased, surprised, and embarrassed. He was surprised that his interest in Leon's activities should matter to Leon, pleased at Leon's token of affection, and embarrassed because he had earned it falsely. He only wanted to go to the baseball field so that he could sneak off to the town offices without anybody knowing about it.

Todd sat in the back of the station wagon, leaning against the rear seat behind his brothers and facing backward. As usual, he had to watch where they'd been instead of where they were going. He was trying to figure out what to do about the rowboat. It was sure to get overlooked in Dad's long list of weekend activities.

Besides fixing the lawn, Mom wanted Dad to work on their income tax today. That would take him forever. So would reading the Sunday *Times* tomorrow. Sunday afternoon Dad and Mom were going to a reception at the museum. Todd wondered if he and his brothers could launch the rowboat alone.

Leon and Michael were talking their father's ear

off about what their baseball coach had said and how the lineup was changing and whether they'd get to go to Atlanta this summer as last year's winning team had. Dad wasn't saying much in response. The narrow country road unreeled in a long green alley behind the car.

"Hey, Dad," Todd put into a breathing space between his brothers' chatter. "How about the rowboat? Can't we get it out of the garage today?"

"Sorry, Todd. It'll have to wait."

"We could get it out ourselves," Leon said. "Some of the guys are coming over this afternoon. Four of us could handle it easy."

"No doubt, but I want to make sure of your seamanship before I let you loose on the river."

"Boy, Dad," Leon said, "you never have time to do anything that's fun!"

Todd remembered the lawn repair job and asked, "Leon, do you think you and me and Michael could help Dad fix those ruts on the lawn? *Then* he'd have time left for the boat."

Leon turned around and eyed him narrowly. "What's with you today? You take some kind of goody pill?"

"Those ruts are so deep, I'm going to have to add soil before I seed them," Dad said.

"We could dig up sod from the river edge and sod it," Leon said. He never could resist getting involved when a job needed doing.

"Well, if you think you can," Dad said grudgingly. "I want the job done right. It's —"

"Don't worry, Dad. Michael and me can do it," Leon said.

"And me," Todd said.

"Yeah, and Todd," Leon agreed, including Todd as an afterthought.

It wasn't hard to slip away from the spotty crowd made up mostly of parents who'd come fully equipped with toddlers and dogs and babies in strollers to watch the ball game. Once the game started, Leon was concentrating too hard on his pitching to notice who was on the sidelines, and Michael was watching two teenage girls chasing a dog back in the outfield where he was stationed.

The town offices were in a low brick building not far from the ball field. As soon as Todd entered the paneled hall, he was faced with a choice of doorways, most forbiddingly closed. An arrow pointed toward the county clerk's office, which was the only door open. A lady behind a counter there directed Todd to the tax assessor's office.

There he had to work up the courage to knock. A rumble answered Todd. He knocked again. The rumble got louder. He opened the door cautiously, poised for a fast getaway if need be. A very fat man at a very small desk covered with papers glared at him.

"I said, come in." The man's voice rose from the volcanic depths of his huge body. "I don't want to buy any raffle tickets, candy for good causes, or tickets to things I never plan to go to for good causes either," the man said. "You a Boy Scout?"

"No, sir."

"Cub Scout, some other kind of scout?"

"No, sir," Todd said.

"Ball player — Little League, church youth group, whatever?" the man asked suspiciously.

"I just want to find out about an island. They sent me to you."

"They did, hey?" the man said. "What do you want to find out about an island?"

"Whether anybody owns it."

"Just out of general interest? You just want to know who owns it?"

"If nobody owns it, I'd like to claim it, please," Todd said.

The man sat still as a photograph. Then he set down the papers he was holding and began to heave with silent laughter. Todd was fascinated watching all the rolls from his chin down his chest to his belly shake. Finally a "hee hee" leaked out. The man wiped his eyes and his face with a clean pocket handkerchief.

"Well," he said. "Well, that's the best I've heard yet. How old are you, kid — eleven, twelve?" Todd nodded. "And you're thinking of claiming an island, eh? You kids today! . . . What for?"

"So I can camp on it."

"Can't you camp on it without owning it?"

"But that'd be trespassing," Todd said.

The man nodded. "It certainly would. You're a law-abiding boy. Well, that's a point in your favor. Where is this island?"

He used the desk to push himself to his feet and walked to a wall-sized aerial photographic blowup of the town. It showed the river clearly, even the ripples out in the middle. Houses appeared as square rooftops, some dark, some light, strung out in the patterns of developments or spotted like street lamps along roads. Even the white, foaming edge of the rapids alongside the lock downriver from Todd's house was visible. The lock looked like a pair of dark dittos.

Todd said, "The island's right in front of my house on the river, but I'm not sure which square is my house."

"What's your address? We got a card to match every parcel of land in town, and that'll tell us who owns it all the way back to the Indians."

A minute later the tax assessor laid a plump finger on a roof. "This here is your house," he said. "But I don't see any island, do you?"

"No," Todd said. "But there's one there."

"Kind of a mystery, huh? Can you figure out how it could be there and not here on this map?"

"Maybe it's not a photograph? It's somebody's drawing?"

"Good try, good, but you missed it. No, this photograph was taken five years ago. Cost the town a pretty penny too. Your island is probably just a sandbar the river threw up since."

"But it's got a tree on it and grass," Todd said.

"Yes, well, grass doesn't take any time to grow. A tree, now — how big is it?"

"A little taller than me."

"Well, it could be two, three years old," the tax assessor estimated.

"But can I claim the island?" Todd asked breathlessly.

The man did his silent heaving laugh again. "I don't know," he said. "I can see a grown man wanting to get away from it all, but a kid your age — What do you want to get away from?"

"My brothers."

"Your brothers? What do they do to you?"

"Plenty."

"I see. Well, you understand that island is likely to disappear one of these days. The river will take it away, just like it built it up. Maybe a flood or a storm or just a wet spring. But so long as it's there, I don't see that anyone's going to mind your taking charge of it."

"Can I put in an official claim so no one can take it away from me?" Todd asked.

"You'd have to maintain it, keep it clean, make good and proper use of it."

"Yes, sir."

"Because we don't want to turn public property over to private use and have it become an eyesore. I don't want phone calls coming in from irate citizens about the scenery being spoiled."

"I'll take good care of it," Todd promised, looking the tax assessor in the eye.

"All right, then." The man's eyes squeezed shut and Todd thought he was going to laugh again, but instead he moved lightly over to a file cabinet. "Let's see now. Seems to me I have some kind of form here that fits. 'Course, you being a minor, it's not going to stand up in court, you understand. But for the purpose at hand — Here it is." He read aloud. "'The undersigned,' that's you. Sign here." He handed Todd his pen. "'. . . is hereby laying claim to the property owned by the State Department of Transportation and described hereinafter as follows.' Now you describe the island in your own words right there."

Todd described the island as shaped like a shoe and having a tree on it and being in front of property owned by Mr. and Mrs. Warren Lewis, about twenty feet off their shoreline. "All right, now," the tax assessor said. "I'll keep this on file here so I'll know who to get after if we run short on tax money this year." He smiled hugely. "Shake, son. You're now a landowner, semiofficially, and I wish you luck with your island."

"I'll be careful with it," Todd said. "Can I have a copy of that form I signed?"

"Right you are. Got to hang on to important legal documents." With a single shake of his belly, the tax assessor tore off the bottom sheet of the three and handed it to Todd. It was not too legible, but it made Todd feel secure to have the pink sheet folded in his shirt pocket.

He returned to the ball field in time for the last inning and watched Leon pitch a hitter out.

"Hurray, Leon!" Todd jumped up and yelled in an excess of good humor. "Yay, yay, yay."

Leon looked over at him and grinned. Neither he nor Michael even asked if Todd had been there the whole time. Mother came promptly at twelve. Todd squeezed in among the bags of food crammed in the rear of the small hatchback. Leon and Michael sat up front with Mother.

"Did you have a good game, boys?" she asked.

"Wicked good," Leon said.

"And how was your morning, Todd?"

"Excellent," Todd said thinking of the fat man and the signed claim in his pocket.

After lunch, Leon set to work on the lawn, with Michael and Todd following his direction uncomplainingly. Leon cut out one-foot squares of soggy lawn with his hunting knife and used the square edged shovel to lift each piece up with enough dirt attached to allow the grass to root easily in the new location. Michael prepared the ruts in the front lawn by filling in the deepest parts with loose dirt dug from the back of the rosebed. Todd transported

60

the sod in the wheelbarrow to the front yard, where he and Michael fitted it into place. By the time their father got home, the job was done.

"How's it look, Dad?" Leon asked eagerly.

"Not bad, not bad at all." Dad peered at the reasonably level expanse of sodded lawn. He nodded approval.

"Can we get the rowboat out now?" Todd asked.

"All right. Let's do it before I put my car in the garage."

Todd exulted silently. Today he had gotten everything he wanted, the island, the transportation to it — everything! Now, if only Leon didn't get too interested, and Louie didn't manage to turn his peaceful sandbar into a battleground, it would all work out. Maybe.

Chapter 6

The boat launching went smoothly. Dad helped them carry the wide-bottomed wooden rowboat with three slat seats down to the river. He took the oars over Leon's protest that he was a good rower. Leon and Michael sat on the wide stern seat. Todd had the narrow bow looking backward. It was the third time that day he'd sat backward, but he didn't let it bother him, not when everything was working out so well.

Dad didn't row very far. He took them out beyond the island, toward the middle of the river, where the ripples of the current had showed on the map. "The current's fast here," Dad said. "See how she'll drift if I lift the oars?" He demonstrated while they sat impatiently, waiting to be done with restrictions.

"And don't forget the lock and those rapids are only a mile or so downriver," Dad said. "I want you to row close to the bank, no rowing across."

"Ah, come on, Dad!" Leon said.

Todd only hoped Dad wouldn't say next, "And

Todd, you have to wear a life preserver whenever you're in the boat." That had happened last year, when they vacationed on the shore of Lake Erie, before Todd had passed his YMCA swim class and become a Shark. It had been humiliating to be the only kid on the beach his size wearing a life preserver.

To Todd's relief, Dad didn't single him out for any special precautions today. He talked instead about not standing up in a boat, and about holding on and crouching when you move about, and about tying up to a tree or something stable when you land — all things they already knew. Then he took them back to shore and got a rope out of the garage to use as a painter and, just in case, another rope tied to a life preserver that could be thrown to someone falling overboard.

"A boat," Dad said, "even a rowboat as stable as this one, has to be used responsibly. If I see or hear of any of you kids fooling around in it, you won't use it again."

Leon kept nodding. "Yeah, yeah, yeah." He'd never let Dad's safety consciousness stand in the way of his fun. Michael barely seemed to be listening. He probably wasn't. Michael always relied on Leon to know what was going on. When Dad finally went up to the house to work on his income tax, Todd thought he was probably the only one of the three of them whom Dad had impressed.

"Here comes B.J. and Joe," Leon said to Michael. "Hey, you guys!" he yelled to the two leggy boys hiking down the hillside toward them. "Want to go for a ride on the river?"

"You got a rowboat?" B.J. asked. A brilliant deduction, Todd thought. Leon's friend was good at basketball and otherwise a little dim.

"Let's row down to the lock," Joe said. He had a mustache and looked a lot older than Leon and Michael. Todd had never met him before.

"Nah," Leon said. "Not today. Today we'll just go exploring."

"Exploring what?" B.J. asked.

"Whatever's along the bank of the river here — islands, like that one." He gestured.

"There's nothing on that island," Todd said quickly.

"Who asked you?" B.J. said. "Smart-ass little brothers should wait until they're asked." B.J. bared his teeth at Todd like a baboon.

"I'll row," Leon said.

"Shove over," B.J. told him. "I'll row with you."

The four of them got in. Joe and Michael sat in the stern and Leon and B.J. shared the middle seat and the oars.

"Push us off, Todd," Leon ordered.

"Can I come too?" Todd asked. He felt like a lamb asking to be included in a den of wolves, but he needed to be with them to protect his interests.

He had to make sure they didn't take a liking to his island.

"That's the trouble with little brothers," B.J. said. "You can never get rid of them."

"He can come," Leon said unexpectedly.

Todd grunted and shoved and grunted and shoved, using all his strength to launch the boat made heavier with four big boys sitting in it. When the boat finally slid out of the mud, he scrambled in himself, getting soaked up to his knees.

"Look at the little baby wet his pants," B.J. said.

"Row, B.J.," Leon told him.

Todd sat stiffly in the narrow bow seat. He hated B.J. B.J. would make an even worse big brother than Leon did. B.J. was so mean that Todd was scared of him. He was the kind of kid who liked to torture cats.

"We going to land at this one?" Joe asked pointing to Todd's island.

"Sure, if you want to," Leon said.

"There's nothing on it," Michael pointed out.

"Buried treasure maybe," B.J. said. "Somebody could've dropped a quarter." He laughed at his own humor. Nobody else did.

Todd stayed in the boat watching them tramp all over his island. It didn't take them very long. B.J. shook the tree roughly and Todd yelled, "Hey, leave that tree alone. What'd it ever do to you?"

B.J. shook the tree harder but it didn't break.

"What's the matter, kid?" B.J. said to Todd. "You afraid we might leave you here if you get out of the boat?"

"I'm not afraid of you," Todd said and hoped B.J. believed him.

"He knows Mom would come rescue him," Leon said. "Mom's always looking out for her baby boy."

"Ain't it the truth?" B.J. said. "My bratty little brother gets away with murder and my mom don't say a word. But just let me do one thing — whammo, I get it good." They looked at Todd evilly.

Todd was relieved when they all got back into the boat and rowed on upriver, past their property. He didn't care what they explored now. In fact, if they had gotten near shore, he would have left them and walked home. His mission was accomplished. His island had passed unnoticed.

Just past the farm property next to the Lewis's land, a maze of islands began. Leon spotted a duck blind some hunter had built at the end of a large island and headed toward it.

"Hey, Todd," B.J. said. "You ever want to be Robinson Crusoe?"

"No," Todd said. There were no houses in sight. Only marsh on the land side and islands between that and the main flow of the river. He began worrying.

"This would be a good place to be shipwrecked," B.J. said. "Also a good place to get rid of leeches and little brothers."

"Remember when we left him in the woods that time?" Leon asked Michael. "We told him we were gonna test him to see how good his sense of direction was, and we made him close his eyes and count to a hundred. He was supposed to find his way home then."

"I started out okay," Todd said.

"Yeah, for about three steps. Then you got lost."

"Did he cry?" B.J. asked.

"Nah. He just sat down under a tree and waited till someone came to get him."

"How long did he wait?"

"All day," Todd said.

"He did not. It was just a few hours. Boy, did we get it for losing him!"

"He told on you, huh?" B.J. asked.

"No, I did not!" Todd said.

"He doesn't tell," Michael said.

"My little brother does," B.J. said. "He loves to get me in trouble."

"Sometimes Todd tells," Leon said. "He told about his art project."

"Well, you wrecked it," Todd said.

"We wouldn't have if you'd paid us the ransom money," Leon said.

"Why should I pay a ransom for my own art project?"

"Because we asked you to lend us money for the baseball and you wouldn't, you little wimp," Leon said.

"Why should I lend you my money? I don't even like baseball."

"Then what'd you watch us for this morning?" Leon asked.

Todd shut up. He always said too much when he was excited. The safest thing to do was say nothing at all.

"Cat got your tongue?" B.J. teased. "Little baby."

"I'm not a baby."

B.J. laughed. He had made Todd talk. "You should of seen what I done to my little brother last winter. I fixed it so when he turned on the lamp in our room, he electrocuted himself."

"How'd you know you weren't going to kill him?" Leon asked.

"I didn't know and I didn't care," B.J. boasted.

"I feel sorry for your little brother," Todd said.

"Why? He's just a rotten little kid, like you."

"Todd's not so bad," Michael said.

"He'd be okay," Leon said, "if he wasn't always playing up to Mom and making her think he's so perfect, when we do all the work around the place and he never has to do nothing."

"What are you talking about, Leon?" Todd objected. "That's not true."

"Sure it is," Leon said. "You're a mama's boy."

"A fag," B.J. said gleefully, "a wimpy little fag."

Todd felt wormy with anxiety. He had heard a resentment in Leon's voice that he didn't understand, and B.J. was out to get Todd, no question. If

B.J. could talk Leon into it, Todd wasn't going to escape this boat ride unharmed.

"I never did anything to you," Todd said to Leon.

"This would be a good boat to fish from," Michael said. "Want to go fishing tomorrow, Leon?"

"Hey, that's a good idea," B.J. said.

Todd listened to their plans with half an ear. He wondered if Michael had intentionally changed the subject. Todd hoped so. It would mean Michael, at least, liked him — a little anyway. Todd didn't know why Leon hated him. Bad as Leon was to him, Todd admired his brother, especially the way he could do anything he put his hand to without being told how. If Leon were stuck on a desert island, he'd build up a whole civilization with no trouble, while Todd would probably need a stack of instruction books just to get started.

Leon and B.J. had turned the boat around and were rowing back toward home now. A good thing, too, because the sun was already getting down near the horizon, and the brightness was gone from the river. They came abreast of the island with the duck blind on it, and B.J. said, "I once found a full six-pack of beer in a hunter's blind like that one."

"You want to stop and see if anything's there?" Leon asked.

"Yeah," B.J. said. "Pull up to shore. You can send your little brother to check it out. Make him useful for something."

B.J. lifted his oar. Leon paddled with his, and the

boat obediently swung around and nosed into the thick, yellow grass bank of the island. "Go on, Todd," Leon said. "Hop out and check out that blind."

Todd considered. Did they really want to see if anything was there, or was this a trick? He looked at Leon's impassive face and B.J.'s leering one. "Someone else can do it," Todd said. "I don't want to."

"Oh, mama's baby doesn't think he wants to," B.J. mimicked.

"Go on," Leon said. "What's the big deal?"

"I don't want you to leave me here," Todd admitted.

B.J. laughed uproariously. "He's chicken! God, is he a little chicken baby."

"We won't leave you," Leon said.

Todd could see it was important to Leon that Todd obey him. It was a matter of face. Leon had to show he was in command. Reluctantly Todd looked toward the blind, hesitating.

"If he doesn't want to go, we could carry him," B.J. said.

"Leave the kid alone," the silent one, Joe, said suddenly.

Todd looked at him with gratitude. "Okay, I'll go," Todd decided.

"Then hurry up. We haven't got all night," Leon said.

Todd let himself down slowly into the grasses. It

was getting pretty chilly now that the slanted light of the setting sun was all that was left. He felt his sneakers filling with cold water again. He crouched and ran as well as he could to the end where the screenlike blind has been built. He looked back over his shoulder. The others were still there. Quickly he looked on the sheltered side of the blind away from the river. There were just some cigarette butts and cartridge shells.

"Nothing here," he yelled.

"Come on, then. It's getting late," Leon said.

Todd hurried back to the bank, but when he got there, the boat was drifting backward, two feet, three feet, four feet from shore. "You promised!" Todd cried in outrage.

The four faces stared at him. He couldn't read sympathy in any of their expressions. "Can you swim, kid?" B.J. taunted.

"Come on, Leon, you promised him," Michael said quietly.

"You better not leave me here." To his dismay Todd's voice was shaking. "I'll tell this time. You better believe I'll tell!" He didn't want to shiver on this island all night, waiting for his parents to search the river for him. "I'll get you in such trouble! You won't go anywhere for a month," he yelled in sudden fury. He'd never done anything to Leon. Why was his brother treating him like this?

Todd was crying when Michael said from close by, "Get in, Todd. Come on."

They'd rowed the boat silently back to shore. Humiliated by his own tears, Todd climbed aboard. As soon as they touched land in front of their own house, he stumbled out of the boat and slogged up the hill. He went upstairs without a word to his mother and stayed in his room staring at the lighted, seemingly placid world of his fish tank. He knew even that world was deceptive. Big fish ate little fish; tails got chewed in fights; and the stronger got the food before the weaker had a chance at it. What had happened wouldn't have made him feel so bad if it hadn't been his own brother.

Michael appeared at the door and said, "Mom says come down for dinner now."

"How come Leon hates me?" Todd asked.

"Leon doesn't hate you."

"Yes, he does."

"He just thinks you're a show-off," Michael said.

"Me?"

"Yeah, 'cause you're always reading instead of watching TV, and you do so good in school."

"He does good too."

"Not all the time, like you. And besides, Leon thinks you're Dad's favorite."

"Me? *Dad's* favorite?"

"Yeah, I know. I don't see it either. Come on, we got to eat dinner now."

"Michael, do you like me?"

"Sure, you're my brother, aren't you?"

Todd mulled that one over as he followed

Michael down the stairs. It wasn't what he craved especially — to be liked just because he was a brother. Why couldn't Michael like him for himself? He mulled over what Michael had said — that Leon thought he was a show-off. That wasn't fair. It wasn't his fault he'd won that prize in math or that he got A's and outstandings on his report card. He happened to like school-type things instead of sport- and work-type things, that was all. Dinner was fish. He hated fish unless it was fried. This wasn't fried.

"Todd, stop picking at your food and eat," Mother said.

What had begun as a real winner of a day had turned out badly. Just as Mom started slicing the chocolate layer cake for dessert, the telephone rang. Leon ran to answer it. He came back to the table with a surprised look on his face. "It's a girl for you, Todd."

"A girl?" Dad asked.

"You got a *girlfriend*?" Michael asked.

"What's wrong with Todd having a friend who's a girl?" Mother demanded.

It was Louie. "Listen," she said. Todd pulled the receiver away from his ear a few inches because her voice was so loud. "This morning I slapped flyers on every post and bush in the neighborhood. Wait till I show you. They're beautiful, all different colors. My Dad let me use his paper."

"What did you say?" Todd asked her.

"I told them to be at your backyard at two o'clock sharp tomorrow afternoon if they wanted to join an exclusive island club for members only."

"Tomorrow? You told the whole neighborhood to come here *tomorrow*?"

"Yeah, why, something wrong?"

"No," he said. "I guess . . . But what are we going to do with all those kids? I mean, that island can't hold more than three or four people." He could envision hordes of kids milling around and trampling Dad's precious lawn. "What are we going to say to them? We ought to have a meeting and decide first."

"Did you get the rowboat?" she asked.

"Yeah, and the island's mine. I got an official paper to prove it."

"That's excellent, Todd. We're really rolling on this thing. That's terrific. You're my kind of partner. Listen, don't worry about a thing. I'll do all the talking. I'm the president, after all."

"Yeah, but Louie, we better put a limit on how many —"

"No limit. This is a democratic exclusive club. Everybody who wants to can join. We'll find something for them all to do. Listen, I'll bring the flag and we can plant it."

"No," Todd said. "We can't plant that flag until we have some way to defend it. My brother Leon sees that flag flying, he'll tear it down and make me eat it."

"Okay, okay. Whatever you say. Boy, this is going to be great! I'm so excited I bet I don't sleep a wink tonight. Hey, I'll borrow my father's bullhorn from when he had a yacht! That way they'll all be able to hear me."

One thing Todd was sure of — they'd all hear her, bullhorn or not. "Listen, Louie," he said. "Just remember, you can be president, but this is my island." Already he could feel pangs of loss. What he'd meant to be altogether his own was becoming somehow hers and an anonymous theirs as well, not to mention the enemy threat when Leon found out about his little brother's territory.

Todd worried his way back to the kitchen to eat his chocolate cake, only to find the frosting was gone from the piece his mother had saved for him. "Who stole my frosting?" he yelled. Leon and Michael snickered.

"That was mean," Mother told her oldest sons. "Next time we have cake, Todd gets the frosting from yours."

Leon and Michael didn't even protest. Why should they? Who could enjoy gooey frosting three layers deep? Gloomily, Todd ate his dry cake and wondered if tomorrow would be fun or bad news. How had he gotten involved with a character like Louie anyway? He couldn't help having the brothers he had, but he didn't have to get stuck with her.

Chapter 7

The next afternoon his parents got dressed up and went off to the reception for the new art exhibit at the museum. "We'll be back by five at the latest," Mother had assured Todd as if he might mind being alone. Actually, he was glad none of his family would be around to witness the crowd gathered on their back lawn at two o'clock. Leon and Michael had biked over to the school playground to practice shooting baskets with B.J. Their fishing trip had fallen through. "You could go play basketball with them, couldn't you?" Mother had asked Todd.

"Mom, I can't keep trailing around after Leon and Michael all my life," Todd had said and added, "Besides, I may have some people coming to see me about something this afternoon."

"Oh? Friends?" She sounded so pleased. Todd knew he'd never convince her that sometimes he enjoyed doing things alone. In any case, that wasn't his plan for today.

As soon as his parents drove off, he hurried down

to the river, eager to inspect his island up close for the first time. He rowed himself across the quiet strip of water. The boat was easy enough to handle with just him in it. He dragged it up on the heel of the shoe-shaped island and for good measure, tied the painter to the skinny tree. The tree could use a dose of fertilizer, he thought, and patted its trunk protectively.

Next he paced off the length and then the width of his domain. It measured eleven yards long and four yards wide, thirty-three feet by twelve, just enough space for him to pitch a tent. He could bring the star chart he'd always meant to study and a flashlight to read it by and spend clear nights teaching himself to recognize the constellations. He could even keep a log to record bird sightings, and also what boats passed by during the summer, when there was supposed to be a lot of river traffic.

When they'd lived in Ohio, he had considered building a weather station. This island would be a good place on which to leave water-collecting containers to measure rainfall. He could set up a wind sock and measure the force of the wind and its direction. Maybe he'd plant some bushes too, to hold down erosion and attract birds. There were so many things he could do with an island of his own. He almost regretted letting Louie make him go public. She'd tempted him with her idea of building a permanent structure. He couldn't do that alone.

The river on the outside of the island threw up

white lips of foam every few yards. The water glittered with sunshine out toward the middle where it reflected the sky. All along the riverbank, buds on the tips of bare branches were bursting with life, furry buds and feathery ones in gray and green and hard red cones. Even on this small sandbar, the variety of life amazed Todd. He was staring at a native inhabitant, a shiny turquoise beetle trundling under a twig, when he heard Louie hail him.

"Todd, what are you doing out there? Come on back. We only got half an hour till they come."

He looked at Louie, bullhorn in hand, togged out in a red, white, and blue jogging suit with jacket unzipped to show a T-shirt that had a picture of Wonder Woman on it. Louie! His happy solitude was about to end with a bang. How had he gotten himself into this? He hated crowds, and now he was about to be host to a mob in his yard and maybe crawling all over his island. Reluctantly, Todd got in the rowboat and returned to shore.

"Louie," he said. "Let's call the whole thing off, huh?"

"You crazy or something? We can't call it off now. Listen, don't worry about a thing. I'm going to handle it. All right, everybody, can you hear me?" she bellowed through the bullhorn.

Todd covered his ears and complained, "The whole town can hear you. Cut it out, will you?"

"This is a great place for a meeting," she said, ignoring him and surveying the hillside. "I can stand down here and everyone will still be able to see me. You got anything we could serve for refreshments?"

"No," Todd said. "Now listen, I want to limit the members."

"What for?"

"Because we only need five or six. More than that and it's going to be a mess."

"Five or six? You're crazy. A dozen at the minimum. We got a fort to build, buddy boy, and then we need kids for guard duty and communications experts and defenders. We got to have weapons too. I know how to make slingshots. We can make piles of slingshots and there's plenty of rocks around."

"No slingshots. You want to put somebody's eyes out?" Todd protested.

"Well, something softer then, nuts maybe. I'll buy a bag of walnuts in the shell."

"You're the one who's crazy," he said.

Louie ignored that. She was thinking. "Tell you what," she said. "We'll just take the strongest-looking kids, male or female, anybody who looks like they could tote a railroad tie or man a fort and throw a good mudball."

"No wars! This is a peaceful island. It's my island and I say it's going to be peaceful."

"Okay, okay. Don't get excited." She grinned at him, showing a dimple in her cheek. "You're kind of cute when you get excited, Toddie boy."

"Listen, Louie, you call me Todd. Just Todd, nothing else," he said firmly.

"Yes, sir." She saluted. "So what do you want me to tell them?"

"About what?"

"About the rules of our club."

"Rules? There aren't going to be any rules." Rules weren't any fun. Todd knew that from living with his father.

"Come on," Louie said. "Every club has rules. We'll make ours easy. Like anyone who hasn't helped build the camp, can't be a member."

He considered. "Okay," he said. "That's fair."

"And about dues —"

"No dues," Todd said.

"But we need money to pay for supplies," she said. "Like take bug juice. When I get anywhere near a river, I need a lot of bug juice or I get bitten to pieces."

"You supply your own," Todd said.

"But we'll need things like a walkie-talkie for contact between headquarters and the guard on duty."

"Louie!"

"Okay, okay. So all they have to do is be strong and willing to work. What else?"

"What do they get for joining?" Todd asked. "I mean, why should they want to join?" He had in mind the rights and privileges of using the island.

But Louie said, "All they get is membership," as

if that was enough. "And they have to accept me as president."

"Suppose they want to vote?"

"Hey, Todd. You promised me. I've got to be president. I've just got to be."

"Don't worry," he said. "I was just supposing. You'll be president."

They decided that membership would entitle a person to attend all club meetings and events like campouts and parties. Louie suggested that the first event should be a flag-raising ceremony after the fort was built.

Todd began to warm to the idea of having his own club. He didn't like all the compromising that was necessary when you did something with other people. It was a lot easier to have nobody to suit but yourself. On the other hand, people contributed surprises that made a project more interesting.

"You any good at constructing things?" Louie asked idly when they'd sat down on opposite sides of the beached rowboat to finish waiting.

"Fair, I guess. I've never built much. My brother Leon does all the building."

"I was thinking about it," Louie said. "And I can't figure out how we're going to attach the roof after we get the railroad ties stacked up."

"I could ask my father for some ideas," Todd said uncertainly. The trouble with asking for Dad's advice was that Dad never came up with simple suggestions. Any way he wanted to do a thing was always complicated and hard. Then usually once you'd asked his advice, he wouldn't let you do it your way anymore. "Let's get the walls up; then we'll worry about the roof," Todd said.

"You got a watch?" she asked.

"Yeah. It's two o'clock."

"How come nobody's here, then?"

"Relax," he said. "People always come late." She looked so eager, sitting there perched on the edge of the boat and already smiling a welcome for the first arrivals, that he began hoping kids would start showing up. Minutes passed. Louie fidgeted. Todd reassured her even while his own doubts grew.

At two twenty, a scrawny little kid who looked about seven years old marched past Todd's house and down the hill toward them. He wore only a dirty T-shirt and jeans, even though it wasn't above fifty degrees and was windy besides. He had a pinched face and a skimpy body.

"Is this where to come for the island club?" the kid asked.

"No," Louie said. She glowered at him as if it were his fault nobody else had come. "You're too young. We need big, strong kids who can lift heavy things in this club."

"I'm strong," the kid said, not fazed by her put-down.

"You're too young anyway," Louie insisted. "Look, it's no go, kid. Find somebody your own age to play with."

82

Todd winced at Louie's blunt rejection. Why make the kid miserable? Wanting to let him down gently, Todd asked, "Just how old are you?"

"I'm ten and a half. I go to Saint Agnes. Sixth grade."

"Ten and a half?" Todd said and looked at Louie. They couldn't disqualify the kid for being half a year younger than they were.

"Wanna see me lift something?" the kid said. He looked around without waiting for an answer, and seeing nothing liftable, said, "You guys stand up for a second." No sooner had Louie and Todd stood than the kid crouched and heaved up the bow of the rowboat. When he had it well off the ground, he looked at Todd and asked, "How's that?"

"Good," Todd said. "Excellent. You're strong, all right. Hey, put the boat down, okay?" He didn't want the kid to wind up with a hernia. "What do you say, Louie?"

"Come here." She gestured to Todd. They huddled for a conference far enough away so the kid couldn't hear.

"Listen," she said, "I don't care how strong he is. Nobody's going to want to join our club if it looks like we got nothing but losers in it."

"He's the only kid who's showed up so far," Todd said. "I say let him in."

"But it's early yet. You said yourself nobody ever gets anywhere on time." She sounded so disappointed. Todd understood that it wouldn't be much fun for Louie to be president of just the little kid and him.

"I don't get it," she said, looking over her shoulder at the hilltop. "I put those signs up everywhere."

"Maybe something else is going on today that everybody went to," Todd said.

"So can I join?" the little kid called.

"You're in," Todd told him. "What's your name?"

"Hank. What's yours?"

Todd introduced Louie and himself and told Hank what they were planning to construct on the island. He didn't mention wars or enemies.

Hank nodded. "Then what, after we get this place built? What's it for?"

"Oh, we can use it for campouts," Todd said.

Hank looked doubtful. Finally he said, "I guess it would be a good fishing place. I like to fish." That seemed to decide it for him. He sat on the other side of the boat from Louie, and they settled down to waiting again.

Minutes dripped by. The warm sun on his shoulders made Todd drowsy. Louie's smile was drooping, dropping, gone. It was almost three o'clock, and still she stared hopefully at the top of the hill. To avoid feeling sorry for her, Todd tried to talk to Hank.

"Aren't you cold in just that T-shirt?" Todd asked him.

"I don't get cold."

"You come from the neighborhood back of Louie's house? Key's Road development?"

"Yeah."

"Any other kids in your family, Hank?"

"Yeah, lots. We got six kids in our house."

"Boy, that is a lot." Todd wondered how much time you had in the bathroom with five other kids needing it too. And what happened to a chocolate cake if you came to the table two minutes late?

"It's nice and quiet here by the river," Hank said.

"Nobody's coming," Louie said in a voice like a foghorn.

"Three of us is enough to carry those railroad ties," Todd consoled her.

Louie exploded in a burst of swear words. "Nothing ever works out right for me," she mourned.

Todd and Hank exchanged glances. Todd wasn't thrilled with Louie's use of words that always made his mother wince when anyone slipped and used them in her hearing. Nevertheless it surprised him that Hank spoke up.

"Girls shouldn't use them words," Hank said flat as an iron on a board.

Louie whipped around to glare at Hank. "Who asked your opinion?"

"You shouldn't use them words," Hank repeated.

Hank should be a minister someday, Todd thought. He'd never heard anyone sound as sure of right and wrong.

Louie turned her back on both of them. "Pip-

85

squeak," she muttered.

"Listen, Louie," Todd said. "We can have more fun with just three of us than if it was a whole crowd."

"I *wanted* a crowd," Louie said. "I wanted to stand up and be a leader for once. When my dad was a kid, he was always the leader."

"You want to forget the whole project then?" Todd asked her.

She looked at him, then looked toward the island, sweeping in Hank and the rowboat for good measure. "Oh, what the hell," she said. "Might as well go ahead with it."

"I told you not to use bad words," Hank said patiently.

"Okay, okay. I'm sorry." Louie stood up. "Listen, you guys, we'll meet at my house after school tomorrow, and we'll start moving out those railroad ties. Right?"

"Right," Todd said. Outrageous as she was, he was glad that Louie was going to stick it out. Developing the island with just the three of them didn't make him anxious, the way a whole crowd of strangers would have. It would still be mostly his place, and besides, there'd be someone on his side when Leon found out what was going on.

Chapter 8

Hank turned out to be a pint-sized superman. With the help of a wheelbarrow, he and Todd and Louie could heave up one railroad tie at a time and transport it down Louie's long driveway, across the road and down the slope of Todd's lawn to the river. Then they ferried the tie to the island aboard the rowboat. But it was slow work, and Todd worried aloud about the ruts the wheelbarrow was making in the soft, wet bottom of his father's lawn.

At the end of the first afternoon, Monday, Todd could feel every pound of the four railroad ties they had transported to the island in his aching shoulders. He wondered if Louie and Hank suffered too but wasn't about to expose his weakness by asking, especially since neither of his working partners complained.

In fact, Louie was in her element. She snapped out endless orders none of them needed. "Shove it this way. Watch it doesn't tip. Heave up. Here we go." She was more bossy even than Leon, but as Todd wasn't obliged to follow her orders unless he felt like it, he didn't let them bother him. Hank didn't seem to mind her either. He was a silent, steady worker, intent only on getting the job done.

Todd was neither silent nor uncomplaining. "It's going to take us forever," he said after they stopped work and surveyed the results of their labor — a crosshatch of dark-colored wood barely visible on the island.

"So what? What else do you have to do that's better?" Louie asked. "At least we're building something."

"Yeah," Hank said. "It's gonna be a solid clubhouse."

Todd thought he personally would rather be reading a good book than doing all this hard labor, but he kept that to himself. After all, it was his island and his idea on which they were spending themselves.

"Same time tomorrow," Louie said.

"Aye aye, Captain Bligh," Todd said. Hank just nodded and trotted off. How did the little kid have the energy left to run, Todd wondered. He dragged himself into the house and groaned when Mother asked him to take the garbage down to the garage.

"What're you building out there?" Leon asked when they all sat down to dinner. The island was cloaked in the darkness of the riverbanks under the pale evening sky.

Todd tensed. Leon had noticed. This was the danger point. "A clubhouse," Todd said.

"With those far-out kids?" Leon looked amused.

"Leon," their mother said. "Don't be rude. Todd doesn't criticize your friends, does he?"

"You're building a clubhouse?" Dad asked. "Where?"

"On the island just off shore," Todd said.

"I don't want our backyard messed up," Dad said. "I'm going to have enough of a problem making that scruffy grass into a decent lawn as is."

"I'm being careful," Todd said.

Unfortunately for Todd, the skin on the chicken Mother took out of the oven just then didn't look crisp enough to suit them. The chicken went back into the oven. Michael and Leon went to watch TV. Dad used the waiting time to examine the lower end of his property. When he returned fast, Todd knew he was in for trouble.

"You've made ruts already," Dad accused.

"I'll fix whatever I mess up, Dad," Todd said.

"Since when did you get to be a lawn expert?"

"Warren!" Mother intervened. "This project is important to Todd. Let him see what he can do. Please!" She looked at Dad with a lot of unsaid things in her face.

Apparently he understood, because he let his breath out slowly and said, "You'd better be sure you don't leave me any extra work, Todd. I've already got too much to do."

Leon and Michael came back into the kitchen to see what was going on.

"Is the chicken all right now?" Mother asked, holding the oven pan out for everyone's inspection.

"It's browner," Michael said.

"It's fine," Dad decided and they settled back down to dinner.

"All I can say is Todd sure picks weird friends," Leon said.

"They're good kids," Todd said. "What's so great about your friends, anyway?"

"At least my friends aren't crooks."

"Who's a crook?"

"That Hank."

"Leon! That's a terrible accusation," Mother said. "Can you back it up?"

"B.J. knows the kid. B.J. says the kid was caught stealing," Leon informed them.

"B.J.'s full of it," Todd said.

"That doesn't sound like a very strong case," Mother said. "Just one boy's say-so about another boy."

"Well, and what about Todd's other pal?" Leon asked. "She thinks she's a boy, looks like one, acts like one, and calls herself Louie. What kind of name is that for a girl?"

Todd stood up. "Listen, Leon, you're making me mad. I'm gonna sock you in another second if you keep talking like that."

"Oh, big shot little brother! You're so brave when you've got Mom here to protect you. Go ahead and try and hit me. You know what you'll get back," Leon jeered.

"Both of you calm down now," Mother said. "I don't want to hear another unpleasant word from either of you. Warren, can't you say something to your sons?"

"I'll discuss it with you after dinner," Dad said grimly to Mother. Then, turning to his sons, he said, "In the meantime, we'll finish eating in silence unless you boys have anything pleasant to say."

Mom frowned at Dad and said nothing. Todd and Leon sat down. What's Dad mad at Mom about, Todd wondered. What did *she* do? His parents usually had their arguments in private, so he wasn't likely to find out. Besides Todd had other worries. Leon was going to make trouble for sure. He had already started with his lie about Hank — and that had to be a lie. Hank was a game little guy, too solid and steady to be a crook.

Todd tried approaching the riverbank from different angles, but that just spread the ruts in a wider fan along the soggy lower third of the Lewises' lawn. By Wednesday, when only half the ties were delivered to the island, the lawn looked hopeless. Todd was glad his father was out of town again, back at the trouble-prone power plant installation in Saudi Arabia.

"We've got to do something," Todd said to Louie and Hank. "My dad'll kill me when he sees this."

"We could carry the ties over the last part by hand," Hank said doubtfully.

"Why don't we ask your brothers to help us?" Louie suggested.

"Forget that," Todd said.

"Let's take an ice-cream break and talk about it," Louie said. Todd and Hank agreed willingly. Ice-cream breaks at Louie's house had turned out to be the highlight of the building process.

They trooped through her front door and passed under the elegant crystal chandelier in the center hall. The staircase there was the only part of the house that had brought forth a comment from Hank the first time he saw it.

"Is this a museum?" Hank had asked as he stared in awe at the grand curve sweeping up and around.

By now, they took the staircase for granted, along with the well-stocked kitchen. Todd chose chocolate nougat ice cream today from the four flavors Louie offered them. They busied themselves making sundaes with chocolate fudge or butterscotch topping and nuts and canned whipped cream. Todd and Hank knew where everything was kept by now and got their own ingredients. Hank's sundae had a little of everything on it. Louie took her ice cream plain. Todd used the syrup and nuts. He was savoring the first delicious bite when Louie said:

"Couldn't we just ask your brother Michael and leave Leon out of it?"

"That'd get Leon madder than anything," Todd said.

"Well, we could use both of them. I'll ask them if you don't want to," Louie offered.

"Louie, do you want to be president or not?" Todd said. "Anything Leon does, he always has to be the boss. Soon as we ask him to help, he'll take over."

"How about you, Hank?" Louie asked. "Aren't there any more musclemen like you back home?"

Hank grinned shyly, but shook his head no. He hadn't told them much about his family, not even exactly where he lived. Louie had asked him for his telephone number so she could let him know about any change in plans, but Hank said she didn't need to call him and not to worry about it.

"Could be Hank's a creature from outer space," Todd joked privately to Louie. "That would explain his superhuman strength."

"His mother probably doesn't like taking calls for him or something," Louie said. They weren't curious enough to do more than guess.

Yesterday Todd had asked Hank, "What's parochial school like?"

"You got to be quiet and sit up straight," Hank had said.

"Do they hit you?"

"What for?" Hank looked at Todd suspiciously. "I don't do nothing wrong."

"I know that," Todd had said and felt silly. That was the day after the evening Leon had said Hank was a thief. Todd was still convinced Hank couldn't be. Not only was he dependable and hard-working, but he always came down firmly on the side of good behavior, more so, in fact, than any other kid Todd had ever known.

While they were still attacking the mountainous ice-cream sundaes, Louie said, "Well, any of you guys got an idea, then?"

"We could lay a couple of ties across two long boards and carry them that way," Todd said. "Of course, we'd have to get one of our mothers to help because we'd need four people, one at each end of a board. My mother would be willing except she's working late every day this week."

"Your mother! You'd expect your *mother* to do something like that?" Louie asked. "My mother would faint dead away if I asked her to lift anything heavier than her nail file. She's so helpless she can't even get herself out of bed in the morning. My dad and me do everything around here. We even make our own breakfasts."

"You shouldn't talk about your mother that way," Hank said stiffly. Todd agreed with him, although he didn't consider it his business to tell Louie how to speak about her own mother.

"Listen," Louie said, "you don't know my

mother. All that lady does is play cards and spend money. Even my dad says she's useless."

"But you talk like you hate her," Todd observed.

"I don't hate her," Louie said. "I just don't have any respect for her. All she cares about is how things look. 'Louanne, wear a dress. . . . Louanne, don't walk like that. . . . Don't talk like that. . . . Lower your voice. . . . Don't you want to be a lady, Louanne?'" Louie got up and minced around the kitchen on her toes with her pinkies stuck out to illustrate what she was saying. "My father says if she wasn't so helpless that she can't even take care of herself, he'd have dumped her long ago."

"Hey, Louie," Todd said, "you shouldn't tell things like that."

"You want to talk mean about your mother, we don't want to hear it," Hank said. He put down his spoon as if he expected Louie to throw him out before he finished his sundae, and he was prepared to leave.

"I can talk about my own mother any way I like," Louie said, not at all upset by their criticism.

"Your mother just wants you to grow up right," Hank said. "Girls are supposed to act like girls."

"Oh, ho! Look who knows all about girls!" Louie chortled.

Hank blushed and said nothing.

"I want to grow up to be like my dad," Louie went on. "He *does* things, and he says when I finish college, he'll make me a partner in his business."

"What about your older brother?" Todd asked.

Louie shrugged. "He'll never come back. Him and my dad never got along." She sounded sorry about her brother.

"Do you like him?" Todd asked.

"My dad? He's great."

"No, your brother."

"Yeah, I like him. I write to him sometimes. He's sort of lonely out there, but if my dad knew I write, he'd hit the roof. He says I'm his son now. He wants to forget my brother was ever born."

"What'd he do?" Hank asked.

"Oh, he got in trouble with the law. He got caught stealing a car," Louie said.

Hank's face turned chalky and his mouth clamped shut. Todd hoped Hank's expression had nothing to do with what Leon had said about him.

When they started outside to resume work, they found it was raining. Nobody objected to Louie's suggestion that they forget the fort for the afternoon and go up to her room to play with her electronic games. For the first time Mrs. Lavoy was downstairs when Todd and Hank were ready to leave.

Louie waved a finger at each boy and said, "This one is Todd and this is Hank, Ma. They're the ones in my club."

"How nice to meet you," Mrs. LaVoy said warmly. "Did Louie offer you some refreshments? Or is it too close to dinnertime?"

Todd mumbled something polite. Mrs. LaVoy

looked just like a mannequin in a department store to him. Everything seemed to be painted on or phony, from her long red nails to her long black eyelashes and high, puffed-out hair. She didn't look anything like Louie at all.

Todd could see why Louie might not get along with her mother, but even so, Louie shouldn't tell nasty things about her. Hank's close-mouthed way about his family was more admirable. That kid had a lot of good qualities. Still, Louie was more interesting and exciting to be with, probably because he never knew what she'd say or do.

Chapter 9

Dad was furious about his lawn. He said it would take him a whole afternoon of rolling it to get it back in shape, and he'd have to rent a heavy-duty roller to do it.

Todd apologized, but his father only looked at him tight-lipped. Then he wouldn't talk to Todd at all. His father's silent anger was harder to endure than any yelling his mother ever did when she got angry. Dad's anger took away Todd's satisfaction in having transported all the railroad ties to his island.

"Can't you talk to him for me, Mom?" Todd asked. "Tell him I didn't mean to wreck the lawn."

His mother looked up from the letter she was writing and gave him a one-armed hug. "Todd, you know I love you very much, and I'd speak up for you to your father in a minute if I didn't think it would make things worse for you."

"Why would it make things worse?"

"Well, your father thinks — that is, he told me the other night, and I think he may be right in a way — that —"

"Mom!"

She sighed and began again. "Your father and I, *we* think that the reason Leon picks on you so much is because I'm always coming to your defense. Leon feels I baby you, and that makes him angry. You understand what I'm saying?"

"So you're not going to stick up for me anymore?"

"Well, not unless you really need me."

"You mean unless they're burning me at the stake or shooting apples off my head?"

She laughed. "You're a big boy now, Todd. You're almost as tall as Leon. Have you noticed that?"

"I'm nowhere near as strong as him."

"Leon's tough, and he does enjoy physical rough and tumble, but the fact is, you probably could defend yourself fairly well if you tried."

Todd nodded. So he was being cut loose from his mother's apron strings. He felt sad to be losing his protector and comforter, but proud that his parents thought he could take care of himself.

"But what can I do about Dad?"

"Nothing, darling. Just be patient. He'll start talking to you again soon."

The long-range weather forecast was for cloudy weather, heavy rains, and wind for the next week. The island looked like an abandoned lumberyard with the wet railroad ties sprawled every which way.

Tuesday the sun defied the weatherman and shone benignly in on Mrs. Harris's free reading class. Todd looked up from an Ursula LeGuin book he was reading and sent Louie a note across the classroom.

"I'll get Hank and come over to your place after school," she wrote back.

As far as Todd knew, Hank just appeared like a leprechaun from the shrubbery at appropriate moments. He wondered how Louie was going to get Hank without knowing where he lived. When he stopped her in the hall on their way to math to ask her, she said, "I know where he lives. I went over to his street the other day and found him."

"You did? He let you in?"

"His mother did. She's nice, kind of fat but friendly. There's kids coming out of the *walls* in that place. I don't know how many brothers and sisters Hank's got. It looked like more than six to me. And the yard's full of broken junk. It's great!" Louie grinned.

"Did you get his phone number?" Todd asked.

"No. The phone's not working. They got behind in the bill or something, but don't worry. I can get over there in a minute by the shortcut."

Idly, Todd wondered if the reason Hank was so secretive was because he was embarrassed about being poor. Todd could tell him that being poor didn't mean anything to his friends. Hank should have seen Louie's face when she was talking about all the kids in Hank's house. It was obvious Louie thought Hank was lucky. She had nobody home but a mother who was either giving herself a facial or having a masseuse in to rub her back. That must be pretty lonely for a girl like Louie who liked action and people.

Todd was beginning to think he liked action and people too, at least in moderation. He'd missed his friends on those rainy days when he hadn't gotten together with them. They might be way-out kids as Leon had said, but they seemed normal to Todd now that he'd gotten used to them.

It started to rain hard again just before the end of class. Todd considered telling Louie they ought to wait to begin building again until the rain stopped for sure. Then he thought, Let Louie be the one to back out. If necessary, he could put on his nylon poncho. Just as he left school, a girl stopped Todd to say, "Louie said to tell you she got detention. She says wait till tomorrow to meet."

"What'd she get detention for?" Todd asked.

Louie's message carrier didn't know, but everyone on the bus did. They were all gleefully recalling the way Louie had told off the music teacher right in the middle of the crowded hall. Todd guessed Louie wouldn't be taking cello anymore.

"That Louie," a kid sitting in front of Todd said. "She's always doing something."

"She's a show-off," a girl across the aisle said.

"She's crazy," someone else added.

Todd wondered if he should defend Louie. Louie's a good guy, he could say, but to whom? Nobody was even noticing his existence. Besides, he didn't want to give them the idea that Louie was his girlfriend or something. She was a friend of his, but not his girlfriend.

He wished Louie wouldn't keep doing these things that made her so conspicuous. It embarrassed him to stick out. Should he speak up anyway? The conversation across the aisle turned to other things. He was already leaving the bus before he decided he should have spoken up for Louie. She was his friend; he should have defended her in public. He was sorry he hadn't. It made him like himself less.

Wednesday the sun shone so energetically all day that the air sparkled. It was a bud-bursting day, full of happy robins yanking up worms and puddles gleaming in the streets. The sky was chased clean of clouds.

"Construction crew reports this afternoon, right Todd?" Louie asked.

"Right. How did detention go yesterday?"

"Okay. Shatzy gave me a lecture. He says I'm basically a dear, sweet girl underneath and I ought to stop giving people the wrong impression." She giggled. "I think I'll switch to the harp."

Todd laughed. "The harp! You?"

"Yeah, me." She frowned. "Why not?"

"No reason." He laughed some more. She punched him hard in the upper arm. "Hey, what'd you do that for?" he asked.

"Because," she said, "you don't laugh at your friends. I don't care who else laughs at me, but my friends don't."

He was impressed by her good sense. When it came to friendship, he knew he had a lot to learn.

Louie appeared promptly at three thirty-five with Hank in tow. All three stood at the top of the hill looking at the island. "You got any ideas on how to stack up those railroad ties?" Louie asked.

"We need help," Hank said.

Todd knew what they were thinking. Leon and Michael were in the house. All Todd had to do was ask them. But he wouldn't. "We could just spread the ties out to make a floor and set up a tent on that to camp out in," he said.

"What about the fort? I thought we were building a fort we could defend from our enemies," Louie said. She sounded angry.

"We're too old for cowboys and Indians," Todd said.

"I don't care," Hank said. "All I want to do is fish. I don't want to camp or play cowboys and Indians either."

"Oh, shut up, Hank," Louie said irritably.

"Louie!" Todd said. "One thing I know about friends is you don't talk to them like that."

Louie made fists and Todd thought he was going to have to choose whether to hit her back as if she were a boy or not hit her back because she was a girl. It was the first time sex had been a problem in their relationship. But Louie untensed and let her fingers droop. "You're right," she said, and she told Hank she was sorry.

"That's okay," Hank said shyly. He flashed a rare smile that was beautiful even though his teeth were crooked.

They went back to staring at the island. It worried Todd that each of them seemed to have a different idea of how to use the island. How could they have a club when everyone wanted something different from it? He glanced uneasily at the pick-up-sticks pile of railroad ties. They could barely heave one onto a wheelbarrow, all three lifting and straining together. How were they going to stack them up as high as their heads for the walls of a fort?

"We've *got* to get help," Louie said as if her mind were in step with his, but one pace ahead.

The rumbling of the wheelbarrow crossing the driveway made Todd turn his head. Leon was trundling a pyramid-shaped evergreen down the lawn.

"What are you doing with that, Leon?" Louie called.

"What's it look like I'm doing?" Leon said and dumped the small spruce, which was about as tall as he was, next to a big hole.

"Can we help?" Louie asked.

"You can bring me that hose back there."

Louie ran eagerly for the coiled hose, turned on the outside faucet, and unwound the hose down the hill. She handed the nozzle end to Leon who turned it on and started filling the hole he'd dug with water. Louie stood talking to him. Todd looked at Hank and in silent agreement they followed Louie down the hillside to hear what she was up to.

"Are you a gardener?" Louie was asking Leon.

"When I get paid to be."

"Mom's paying Leon and Michael to plant a screen of trees on this side of our property," Todd said.

"And not you?" Louie asked.

Todd shrugged. Nobody ever paid him to do anything. He was the baby, but he wasn't going to tell Louie that. "I don't need any money," Todd said. It wasn't entirely true. He needed money for his fish tank, to buy new fish and food and the fast-disappearing greens that kept the fish healthy. It took most of his allowance, but he managed. "Leon likes to work," Todd said.

Louie's eyes widened. "Hey, Todd, come over here," she said and beckoned him extravagantly. They walked out of Leon's earshot. "Let's hire him," Louie whispered to Todd.

"I told you what happens once he gets involved. We'll end up off our own project."

"Not if we're paying him. That would make it

105

different. He won't have any rights to the fort at all."

"Where are we going to get the money to pay him?" Todd asked.

"Don't worry," Louie said. "I've got lots."

Todd hesitated. He needed time to think it over. "Well . . ." he began, looking for a loophole.

Before he could go any further, Louie said, "Great." She strode back to where Leon was plopping the burlap-wrapped ball of dirt at the bottom of the tree into the half-filled hole.

"How much do you get an hour, Leon?" Louie began her negotiations. Todd winced. Why did she always have to hurtle into everything? Was it true that paying Leon to work would make a difference? Todd couldn't help feeling that hiring Leon was like inviting an enemy invasion.

"You think he'll really help?" Hank whispered to Todd while Louie yakked away at Leon.

"I don't know. Sometimes Leon can be nice." Todd thought of the time Leon gave him the carton of plastic army men that Leon and Michael had played with for years and finally outgrown.

Todd had always hankered for that boxful, which had enough men and machines to set up a room-sized field of battle. There were rubber-tired jeeps and tanks with movable tracks and cannons that fired tinfoil balls on a spring action. Not everything was missing parts either. Of course, during last

Christmas vacation, Leon had decided he and Michael hadn't outgrown those army men after all and he'd reclaimed them.

"You can play too," Leon had said when Todd protested. Todd hadn't played with them though. He'd been angry. It wasn't fair to give a person something and then take it back. The only other time Todd could remember Leon being nice to him was when Leon offered to let Todd come along on a fishing trip in exchange for Todd's digging all the worms for Leon and his friends to use. Todd only managed to find a juice can full of worms, but Leon let him come anyway.

"Okay," Louie announced. "It's all set then."

"Wait a second," Leon said. "I said I could do it, I didn't say I would. Who's paying me?"

"What do you care?" Louie asked.

"I'm not taking money from a thief. No way," Leon said.

"Who's a thief?" Louie asked.

Leon pointed at Hank. "Him. That's how he got stuck in a foster family, because his folks couldn't stop him from stealing."

Everyone looked at Hank, who shrank into himself like a whipped dog. In the silence a blackbird serenaded them with clicks and whistles and gravelly trills.

Finally Louie said, "Say something, Hank."

"I don't steal nothing," Hank said.

"Well, but you *did*, didn't you?" Leon asked.

Todd couldn't endure Hank's beaten look. "So what if he did. He's okay now," Todd said.

"How would you know?" Leon asked. "You didn't even know he was a thief."

"Hank's a good kid," Todd said firmly. Again he wished he'd stuck up for Louie on the bus.

"You've sure got funny taste in friends," Leon said. "This one's a thief and that one's a lesie."

"Shut up, you!" Todd's fury came so fast that he rammed his fist into his brother's gut before he even considered what he was going to do.

"Uggh," Leon grunted.

Todd had one instant of satisfaction. He had stood up to Leon! Then Leon began fighting back and Todd was too busy impersonating a human punching bag to feel anything else. In no time, he lay sprawled on the ground with Leon's foot planted on the back of his neck. The grass was stubbly and cold against Todd's face.

"Say 'uncle' or I'll shove your head in," Leon said.

Todd had always had a problem with saying "uncle." He couldn't bring himself to admit defeat even though he knew Leon would release him as soon as he did. Leon's sneakered foot began to push. Todd struggled to rise and twist Leon off. It seemed he had succeeded because Leon fell, but when Todd stood up, he found it wasn't his own efforts that had unseated Leon. Louie was rolling around on the ground pounding at him. Leon seemed to be pounding back at her.

"Hey, she's a girl!" Todd yelled and jumped in to separate the two fighters. With Louie pulling on one side of Leon and Todd on the other, they immobilized him quickly. Leon lay helpless on the ground between them. Todd could hardly believe it. He had Leon at his mercy.

"You want me to knock him out?" Hank asked. He had found a rock from somewhere and was holding it up above Leon's head. It looked about the size of his skull.

"Put that down. He's my brother," Todd said. Decisions were coming to him fast now. Louie was a girl. Leon was his brother, not a real enemy. Hank dropped the rock obediently.

"Listen, Leon," Todd said. "You've got to leave my friends alone."

"I didn't do a thing to your friends."

"You insulted them."

"Okay. I won't anymore."

"Apologize then."

"Why?"

"Because they're my friends and you hurt their feelings."

To Todd's amazement, Leon said, "Okay, I'm sorry. Now let me go."

"Sure," Todd said but he hesitated. "Uh, are you still going to help us build the fort?"

"Let go of me."

As soon as they'd released him, Leon stood up and brushed off his jeans. No way was Leon ever going to work for them now, Todd thought.

"Hey, Leon!" Michael yelled from the top of the hill. "What's going on? You need help?"

"Run!" Louie said. She took off, cutting across the backyard next to the Lewises'. Todd and Hank dashed after her. They kept running all the way across the road and up Louie's driveway to her house.

"Let's get something to eat and decide what to do," Louie said as they arrived at her back door. She was the only one not panting. Todd was so out of breath that he couldn't even answer. He guessed jogging with her father every morning kept Louie in good shape.

They sat around the kitchen table while Louie unloaded a shelf full of meats and cheeses onto it.

"Did you go to jail, Hank?" Louie asked as she set down the container of milk in front of him.

"No."

"Then what happened? Leon was telling the truth, wasn't he? You were caught stealing?"

Hank didn't say anything. He had taken two slices of bread with which to make a sandwich and just sat there holding the bread. He looked sick.

"He doesn't feel like talking about it," Todd said to Louie.

"You don't want to tell us? But we're your friends," Louie said.

"I don't steal nothing," Hank muttered, squeezing the bread.

"Now, you mean. You don't steal *now*. Right? But before —"

"It's wrong to steal," Hank said.

"Then why'd you do it?" Louie persisted.

"Louie!" Todd admonished her.

"Okay, I'm just asking," Louie said to him, and then she turned to Hank. "So how come you didn't even tell us you were living in a foster home? You can talk about that at least, can't you?"

"Louie, *shut up*," Todd said. But it was too late. Hank dropped the bread and took off out the back door.

"What's the matter with him?" Louie asked. "I wasn't saying he did anything wrong. I just wanted to know."

"But *he* knows he did something wrong," Todd said. "And he feels bad about it."

They didn't see Hank again for several days. In the meantime, it started to rain again.

Chapter 10

Thursday morning the river was lashed into foaming white peaks. Todd could just barely see it through the dimming sheets of rain that slapped against the kitchen window.

"It looks like night out," Todd said to his mother.

"I hate driving in this weather," she said as she tied her rain hat under her chin. "You boys be sure to wear your slickers and don't forget to lock up."

Leon was reading the comics page of the newspaper and didn't answer. Michael said, "Don't worry, Mom. We can take care of ourselves."

She blew them a good-bye kiss and hurried down to the garage. Dad, as usual, was out of town; a turbine had failed its on-site test run.

Todd took his cereal bowl to the sink to wash. Leon said, "Your island isn't going to last long in this weather."

"What?"

"I said that sandbar you want to build on is breaking up — or half of it is anyway."

Todd stared out the window trying to determine

if the dark blot that was his island looked any smaller. All he could see in the gust of rain was swirling, opaque grayness.

"Why don't you leave him alone, Leon," Michael said. "The kids worked hard on that island."

"I'm not teasing. I swear!" Leon protested. "I looked out this morning before the rain got so heavy and saw a big chunk gone from the sandbar."

"I don't believe you," Todd said. "That couldn't happen. There's even a tree. That island's lasted long enough for a tree to grow."

"Well, don't cry, little brother. It's not your island anyway."

"Yes, it is. I've got a claim to it."

"What do you mean?" Leon asked. "What kind of claim?"

"I went down to the town offices and put in a claim," Todd said. "It's official. The assessor signed it too."

"You're kidding!" Leon said. "You went and claimed an island all by yourself? I don't believe you."

"Well, I did."

"Oh, sure," Leon jeered and Michael was grinning with disbelief too.

To show them, Todd marched up to his room and retrieved the precious document from behind the fish tank, where he'd hidden it. His brothers studied the barely legible pink sheet in silence. Todd's heart lurched as Leon started to fold the paper. "It's mine," Todd said and grabbed it away from Leon.

"Don't you trust your own brother?" Leon asked.

Without answering the question, Todd repeated stubbornly, "It's mine." He wished he had had the good sense not to show them his document.

The lashing rain stopped as the wind veered off and the sky lightened momentarily. In the clearing, Todd saw the river plainly. Leon was right. The toe end was being gnawed away by the fast-running water. Todd groaned.

"What you ought to do with those Lincoln logs you got out there is build a breakwater to keep off the river," Leon said.

"How am I going to do that?" Todd asked. He was so caught in the misery of losing his island he couldn't do anything but stare out the window at it.

"Well," Leon answered, "what you do is set the logs in the water off the end of the sandbar in a wedge shape, and then you keep dumping rocks and chunks of concrete and like that inside the crib you've made. . . . Want me to draw you a diagram?"

"I can't build a crib with them," Todd said. "We can barely lift them as it is." He was struggling against the tears that were ready to spill. The island was the best thing he'd ever had.

"Not alone you can't, but if me and Michael helped, I bet we could hold that river off all right," Leon said.

Todd looked at his brother suspiciously. "Why would you want to help me?"

"Hey," Leon said. "You're my brother, aren't you?"

Todd nodded.

"And you're not such a bad kid. Nowhere near as much of a jerk as you used to be when all you did was read."

"Thanks," Todd said. Leon's approval stunned him.

"That's okay," Leon said. "Soon as the rain lets up, we'll go to work on it."

"Hurry up," Michael said. "I hear the school bus."

Todd watched his brothers dash out of the house. They weren't wearing their slickers, of course. He put his on thoughtfully. What had he done that made Leon like him all of a sudden? Todd hoped it wasn't just that he'd watched the ball game that Saturday, because he hadn't really watched it, and he didn't want Leon's liking him now to be based on a false notion.

On the other hand, it could be Leon was plotting some kind of trick. He'd looked at that pink sheet from the tax man's office with a funny expression. Todd didn't know what to think.

Even with his nylon poncho, Todd was soaked from the knees down by the time he got to school. Louie was wet from the top of her drenched head to the rubber tips of her sneakers.

115

"How come you didn't wear a raincoat?" Todd asked her.

"I don't mind getting wet," Louie said as she dripped onto the floor.

"You're not wet; you're sopping. Didn't your mother say anything?"

"I told you she never gets up until noon."

"What about your dad?"

"He says if I want to get wet, that's my business. You should've seen him grinning when I ran out this way to catch the bus. He thinks I'm tough as nails."

"Louie," Todd said. "Don't you want to be a girl?"

"Does being a girl mean I have to be weak and helpless?"

"No," Todd said. He sighed and got down to business. "We've got a problem, Louie. The river's chewing up the island. Part of the front end's already gone."

"You're kidding!"

"No, I'm not, but Leon says he'll help us build something to protect it, like a dam wall or something."

"Leon? Your brother *Leon*'s going to help?"

"He says."

"What did you offer him?" she asked.

"Nothing."

"I don't believe it."

"Me either," he said.

116

"Let's take him up on it anyway," Louie said.

By lunchtime the rain had stopped. Louie had to go to a dentist appointment, but she promised to get to Todd's backyard as soon as she could. She suggested that he fetch Hank and drew a map of the shortcut for Todd.

After school, he stopped off at his own house to tell Leon and Michael where he was going. Leon was slugging milk from the container. Between swallows he explained to Michael how they'd plant the railroad ties against the force of the river. When Todd glanced out the kitchen window, he saw a whole tree trunk glide by with branches sticking up like green sails. Odd-shaped debris floated in the tossing waves. It wrenched Todd to see how much smaller his island looked already.

He slogged through the mud between the outbuildings behind Louie's house and found the path through the woods easily. It was damp and piney-smelling. Underfoot the ground was padded with dead leaves from the poplar and pine and birch and swamp maples that made up the strip of woods. Todd emerged onto Hank's street, which was lined with boxy little houses whose neat lawns were decorated with painted deer and wooden windmills. Hank's house looked like a leftover garage sale. Bikes and kids' toys littered the driveway and the backyard. Hank himself answered the door. His face lit up when he saw Todd.

"Hank," Todd said. "We've got problems. The

river's tearing the island apart. Leon's going to help. You coming?"

"Your brother's gonna be there?" Hank asked fearfully.

"Yeah, it's okay."

"You're sure?"

"I think he changed his mind about you," Todd said. Actually he didn't know that, but Leon had suggested Todd summon his friends, and he knew Todd had only two friends.

"I went home last weekend," Hank said.

"Huh?"

"They let me go home to my mother last weekend. My father's not there no more. She kicked him out finally."

"Your real home you mean?" Todd asked.

"That's right. My mother says if I stay good maybe the judge will let me go back to live with her soon."

"What judge?"

"In family court."

Todd didn't know what to say. He was shocked to learn that a judge had the power to remove a kid from his parents' care. "I didn't know they could do that," Todd said, "take you away from your mother."

"If you get in trouble a lot, they can. And if they don't think your family's good enough," Hank said. "You want me to bring anything?"

"No . . . I don't know. Work gloves maybe."

Hank disappeared inside to scrounge up a pair of work gloves. While Todd waited, he considered how lucky he was. No matter how mean his brothers were and how picky his father could be, he'd rather be a member of his family than Hank's or Louie's.

"Got some!" Hank said and held up a pair of white cotton gloves with ribbed cuffs.

Chapter 11

By the time Todd returned to his yard with Hank, the wind had dropped and the sun was giving their backs and shoulders a heat massage. Michael passed them, carrying some frayed gray rope down the hill toward the island, where Leon and his friends B.J. and Joe stood. Todd felt uneasy seeing his island invaded, especially since Michael dumped the rope into the boat and rowed away from shore without Todd and Hank.

"Hey, Michael, bring back the boat," Todd called. Michael ignored him.

"Hey, Leon, I need the boat," Todd shouted.

"Get lost, little brother. We're busy," Leon yelled back and went on consulting with his friends. Todd had to plead with Michael before Michael relented and rowed back to get him.

"Boy," Todd said, "you guys said you'd help — not take over."

"Yeah," Michael said. "But Leon says him and B.J. and Joe can handle it by themselves."

"It's still my island," Todd said.

Michael shrugged, beached the boat, and went to join Leon who was telling his friends, "Look, it's easy. We lower the ties into place from the boat using the ropes. Stack 'em up halfway decent and the current will hold them together for us. Then all we have to do is fill inside with rocks and stuff."

Another few minutes and Leon had his friends convinced that that was the way to go. The older boys behaved as if Hank and Todd were invisible. It frustrated Todd to have to stand by watching, as if he were useless. "Get lost, little brother" — that was what Leon had said to him every time he tried to help with the shack Michael and Leon had built in Ohio two years ago. They'd never allowed Todd near that shack in the woods behind their house. Hadn't anything changed?

He remembered his mother asking, "Can't you let Todd play, too?" and Leon had answered, "Why can't he get his own friends to play with? Why does he have to hang around us all the time?"

Well, Todd *had* his own friends now, and his mother wasn't defending him anymore. He was officially independent and shouldn't still be getting pushed around and ignored.

Louie arrived just as the railroad ties grew into an underwater wall. Already there seemed to be less turbulence close to the toe of the island where the current hit. Todd and Hank rowed Louie to the island.

"Is it going okay?" she asked.

Todd raised his eyebrows. "I guess."

"They're not letting us do anything," Hank said.

Louie stepped out of the boat and strode over to where Leon was readying another tie. "You're doing great, guys. Here, let me help with that end." Louie spoke as heartily as if she were one of the crew.

"Watch out, squirt. We don't need any help," B.J. said.

"You kids could start collecting rocks and fill this crib we're making," Leon said. "We'll need plenty of rocks as big as you can find."

"Really," Louie said and immediately took charge of the younger work party. "Come on, you guys," she ordered. "Let's get a wheelbarrow and go looking."

Finding rocks was no problem. As Todd pointed out, the loose shale that had fallen from the ledges across the road would give them as many wheelbarrow loads as they could handle. They carted load after load down to the river's edge and piled them there, then ferried the rocks over to the island where they had to be dumped into the V-shaped crib by hand.

Filling that crib was slow, exhausting work, and every afternoon after school Todd and Louie and Hank tackled it with no help from the master builders. Todd didn't mind. The island was his, so the labor should be too. It was only when he was feeding his fish on Wednesday evening and happened to check to make sure his pink sheet was in its place that he got upset. The slip wasn't behind the fish tank. He was positive he'd put it back there after showing it to Leon. What had happened to it? Leon!

Todd rushed downstairs to confront his brother, who was doing his math lying on his stomach in front of the TV. "Where did you hide it?" Todd asked.

"Hide what?" Leon's freckled face was guarded.

"The sheet that says it's my island."

"What are you talking about, kid? I didn't hide your sheet." Leon glowered at him threateningly.

"Even if you took it, the island still belongs to me," Todd said.

A sly grin squeezed Leon's bright eyes to slits. "Prove it," he said. The grin convinced Todd. Leon had taken the sheet of paper. Sudden despair weighed Todd down. He hiked slowly back upstairs to think in private.

He couldn't get over it. To have the island stolen by a trick like that! He had expected Leon would try to take it by force, but not that his brother would be so sneaky mean. It made Todd feel helpless. Trickiness wasn't in his nature. How could he deal with it?

For two afternoons and two evenings, Todd sat around brooding. He didn't want to talk to anybody — not his brothers, nor his friends, nor his parents who had made it plain he wasn't to run to them for help against Leon anymore. When Todd finally broke down and told Louie his problem, she advised, "Steal the pink sheet back. That's what you have to do."

"I don't know where he hid it. I looked everywhere," Todd said. "Maybe he threw it away."

"You could take something of his and hide it," Hank suggested when he was informed. "Then he'd have to give you back the island to get his thing back."

Todd considered that advice until he realized that he'd be putting his life in jeopardy if he touched Leon's belongings. Leon could think up something new every day to torment him, and he still wouldn't have his pink sheet back. No, his friends were no help. All he could do was simmer in frustration.

On Friday, Louie sat down beside Todd on the bus on the way home from school. "Snap out of it," she said. "It's still your island."

"No, it isn't."

"Listen to me," she said. "We're going to have a public ceremony. I already called the paper. As soon as we're ready, they'll send a reporter and a photographer, and they'll take a picture of you planting a flag on your island, so the whole world will know it's yours."

"You're crazy. Why should they come to see me plant a flag on an empty sandbar?" Todd asked.

"Leon's going to build us a clubhouse on it."

"Oh, sure!"

124

Louie laughed. "I made a deal with him," she said. "I offered to let him use the Universal fitness machine whenever he wants if he'll help us build a clubhouse. You should have seen his eyes when he saw that gym. He went ape over it. He's already picked stuff from the wood my dad saved from the outbuildings he tore down on our property. He's going to start on the clubhouse this Saturday — with some help from Michael and Hank and me, of course."

Todd shrugged.

"Don't you want to help, too?" she asked.

"What for? It's not my island anymore."

"I just told you. You're going to plant the flag and it'll be in the newspaper that —"

"No," Todd said. "Leon will claim it. It's only my word against his who it belongs to now. I just hope he lets you use the clubhouse after he gets it built, Louie."

"You mean to tell me I went through all this for you and you're not even going to help?" Her voice was so shrill that it pierced the din on the bus. Everyone stopped talking and turned in their seats to see what she was yelling about. Todd slumped in embarrassment. Luckily for him, the bus stopped at their mailboxes right at that moment and Todd hurried off with Louie at his heels.

"Well?" she demanded angrily.

"I'll help," he said.

"Really!" She tossed her curls at him and

marched off without asking him why he'd changed his mind. Good thing she hadn't, he thought. He wouldn't have wanted to admit that he'd help just for her sake, because she was his friend and wanted him to.

Todd had just opened the refrigerator door to see what there was for a snack when the telephone rang. It was Louie. "Listen," she said, "couldn't your tax assessor give you another copy of that paper?"

"Why didn't I think of that?" Todd shouted gleefully. Louie was chuckling when she hung up.

Todd took advantage of his brothers' absence to get out the phone book, locate the number of the town office building, and dial it. The woman who answered said the tax assessor was away and wasn't expected back for several weeks. "Can I do anything for you?" she asked. Todd explained his problem. Then she wanted to know how old he was.

"Eleven," Todd admitted and hastened to assure her, "But he really did give me a sheet that says this island in back of my house is mine. Really."

"Well, I'll look in his files," the woman said dubiously. "Give me your phone number and I'll call you back."

He sat next to the telephone fidgeting for the next half hour. Would she really look? Was she looking now? Or hadn't she believed him? It was rotten to be eleven years old. He wished the phone would ring. Any minute his brothers would barge in.

Before the first ring was over, Todd had grabbed the receiver. "Did you find it?" he asked.

"I'm sorry, honey," the woman said. "I looked everywhere, but it's not in his files. It could be he never filed it. You're sure it was a bona fide claim?"

Todd was sure, but even after thanking the woman for her help, he still had no proof.

That weekend the frame for a simple, windowless building started going up.

"Stacking up railroad ties the way you kids were planning would never have worked," Leon assured them as he sawed two-by-fours for the frame. "You'd have had to drill holes and bolt them together. Otherwise they'd have all fallen down as soon as someone leaned against them."

Todd said nothing. He was still angry at Leon and didn't plan to talk to him ever again. Nevertheless, Todd helped Michael and Louie and Hank lay the leftover ties side by side to make a foundation platform. He rowed back and forth to get the nails; then he and Michael nailed boards across the studs which Leon had firmly planted two feet apart. All week they worked together.

One morning at the bus stop, Louie said, "Maybe the write-up in the paper will get us some club members. And even if it doesn't, at least it'll be right there in print, 'Louie LaVoy, *president* of the Todd's Island Club.'"

"The Todd's Island Club? Don't call it that."

"Why not?"

"It's not my island." He said it bitterly. He could barely recall his old vision of a place all his own where he could go to study the stars and set up a weather station and nobody could get at him. Even before his brother had stolen his island, his vision kept getting blurred in the confusion of everybody else's ideas. That was the trouble with group projects. It was best to work alone if you wanted to accomplish anything.

". . . So what do you think about balloons and soda?" Louie asked him. "I don't want to wind up with nobody coming to the party like last time."

"What are you talking about, Louie?" He had missed some part of what she'd been telling him.

"The flyers," she said. "This time when I put out the flyers, I'm going to offer free stuff to get kids to come."

"When?"

"Saturday, to the flag-raising. Aren't you listening to me?"

"You're going to try *that* again? Why?"

"Because," she said impatiently, "what's the use of being president of a club with just you and me and Hank in it? It's no fun making rules and everything for just the three of us."

"What kind of rules are you thinking of making?" Todd was suspicious.

"Oh, like everybody has to pay me tribute to step foot on the island, and they can only leave if they perform some special feat, like spit a certain distance — say, from the breakwater to the tree. I tried it and I can spit that far — if the wind's right."

"Incredible!" he said.

"Sure," she admitted modestly, taking his remark as a compliment. "That's why I'm president. The leader always has to do things better."

"Being the best spitter doesn't make you the best leader," Todd fumed at her. "Spitting doesn't have anything to do with being president."

He wanted to shake her for being ridiculous, but she only said, "Sure it does," and smiled and got on the bus ahead of him as usual.

He wouldn't sit with her. He was sorry he'd helped build the clubhouse. "Ridiculous," he muttered to himself as he found a seat next to another boy. Todd was leery of publicity ever since that math contest he'd won. When his pictures came out in the paper, adults had congratulated him, but kids his own age avoided him as if he'd done something embarrassing, and he'd wound up feeling like a big show-off, especially when Leon called him one. This seemed too similar a situation for comfort.

That afternoon when they were working alone on the shack, Todd asked Hank if he liked the idea of getting into the paper. Hank was so shy that Todd figured he'd hate the publicity, but Hank surprised him. "Yeah," he said, "Louie said she'd get me in."

"Why do you want to be?" Todd asked.

Hank blushed and ducked his head and answered with his usual cover-up, "I don't know."

All during spring vacation, the shack rose at a steady pace under Leon's directions. He ordered them about and cursed them when they didn't hold a board steady or ruined too many nails whacking them in crooked.

Most humilating for Todd was being sent back to the house for water or cookies or whatever Leon wanted. It made Todd feel like an errand boy instead of lord of his own island. Once Leon even sent him for tissues for Hank's dripping nose, which Leon said disgusted him.

Late in the week, Dad, back home for a few days, peered out the kitchen window and grumbled, "Is that what my lawn was wrecked for?" His eyes were on the clubhouse.

"Isn't it coming good, Dad?" Leon asked.

Their father nodded, which was as close to a compliment as they were likely to get from him.

The final touch was an awning of stiff, transparent plastic in light green ripples that Michael found on a trip to the dump with Mom. The awning had once been attached to a house trailer. Leon said it made a perfect roof. It projected several feet from either

130

side of the clubhouse, and its broken corner barely showed. Michael was so proud of his contribution that he beamed happily at their compliments.

Even Todd felt good seeing the shack finished and standing so sturdily in the center of the island. Instead of a shoe, the island now looked more like a houseboat. It was more impressive than Todd had ever imagined it would be back in the days when it was his. The only bad part was that Leon would probably never let him use it. The island would be just like that shack in the woods back in Ohio.

Chapter 12

Louie had dittoed flyers pasted in the shopping center and the supermarket as well as on the telephone poles in their immediate area. The flyers read:

WITNESS THE FLAG-RAISING ON THE FIRST NEW LAND
CLAIMED SINCE VASCO DA GAMA
*Free soda and balloons at 49 River Road, Saturday
at 11:30 A.M.*

"Why Vasco da Gama?" Todd had asked her.

"I like his name," Louie said. "Aren't you excited, Todd?"

He wasn't so sure. He didn't look forward to a confrontation in public with Leon over whose island it was, and he knew Louie was expecting him to step forward and plant the flag. What would happen if he did was obvious to him. Leon would shove him away, and there'd be a fight between them which would probably be more newsworthy than the story the reporter had come to do. Todd could see the headline now: Brothers Dispute Claim to Island. Little Brother Loses.

The day of the official flag-raising ceremony, the weather was spring perfect — seventy degrees, sunny, and breezy. Louie appeared at ten with a kid's red wagon loaded with two cases of soda, paper cups and three bags of balloons. She wanted something to use as a stand, also pad and pencils for the big club membership sign-up.

Todd offered an old bridge table, which she told him to get while she ran home for the flag she'd forgotten. "Make a banner for the stand," she yelled back over her shoulder. Louie was wearing a tweed jacket Todd had never seen before. It looked much too warm for the weather. Todd had on a T-shirt that said, "Save the Seals." He figured it might make the publicity they were going to get useful for something.

Leon and Michael sauntered down the hill. Their parents had just dropped them off from a baseball game. "Mom and Dad went to buy a new washing machine," Michael told Todd. "They told Leon and me to police the action here."

"It's going to be a mob scene," Leon said. "We're gonna have a yard full of babies coming for the balloons and soda. When's the reporter due?"

"Louie said to look for him anytime," Todd answered his brother. It was one of the few direct exchanges they'd had in a week. Todd was nervous enough to be glad his brothers were there. A yard full of kids was a big responsibility, even if Dad had given up on his lawn for this year.

On the way up to the house for the bridge table, felt-tipped markers, and a ripped up white sheet to make into a banner, Todd saw Hank arriving. At first Todd didn't recognize him. The kid looked like a very small old man in a jacket and tie with his hair slicked down and his narrow face set in serious lines.

"What are you all dressed up for?" Todd asked.

Hank ducked his head. "The newspaper guy here yet?"

"Not yet." So that was it, Todd thought. But why should Hank care so much about getting his picture in the paper?

Michael met Todd as he was lugging the bridge table out the back door. "Louie wants a banner," Michael said.

"I know. I know."

"Well, Leon says to get tomato stakes to attach it to the table and an old sheet and some Magic Markers and some string."

"I got the bridge table; you get the rest," Todd said.

"What are you so grouchy about?" Michael asked.

"Me? Grouchy?" Todd asked angrily. "How would you feel if he was stealing your island in public?"

"Leon's not stealing your island."

"Then why'd he take the paper that says it's mine?"

"I don't know. Why don't you ask him?" Michael said.

"I already did."

"Well, tell him how bad you feel. Not talking to him sure won't do you any good."

Todd delivered the bridge table and stood near the rowboat studying Leon. He was discussing with Louie how to barricade the cases of soda so that kids wouldn't swarm all over them and take what they wanted before they should.

The idea of making Leon see what he'd done, and how much it hurt, hadn't occurred to Todd before. He thought Leon knew he'd scored a direct hit. On the other hand, maybe Leon wasn't any better a mind reader than Todd was. He never knew what was going on inside his friends' heads unless they came right out and told him. But it was too late anyway. Todd was not about to make a public scene, and the public had already arrived.

Three little girls who looked to be about kindergarten age stood shyly watching the banner being attached to the tomato stakes which were then bound to the legs of the bridge table.

"When are you going to sign them up for your club, Louie?" Leon teased her.

Louie ignored him. "Hank, give the girls each a balloon," she said, "and then they can go home."

Hank gravely presented each little girl with the

color of her choice, then stood there patiently blowing up the balloons and knotting them. Instead of encouraging them to leave, this treatment seemed to cement the girls' confidence. They settled down in a row facing the stand as if they were awaiting a performance. Two big dogs flashed down the lawn to join them at the water's edge. One was a plume-tailed setter and the other a black Labrador.

A gang of rowdy kids came tearing around the driveway on bicycles. Todd yelled at them not to use their bicycles on the lawn. To his relief, all seven kids left their bikes next to the Lewises' garage door.

"We came for the free soda," the tallest boy announced. Todd judged him to be his brothers' age, thirteen or fourteen.

"You gotta wait," Todd said, "until after the ceremony. And anyway we're not ready yet. We're just getting set up."

In no time, more than a dozen restless kids were chasing one another around the yard and endangering the new trees Leon had planted along the side. The only ones not in motion were the three little girls. They sat quietly in the midst of the chaos, just looking around them. The dogs barked and chased one another. Louie's checkered flag flapped atop the fishing pole stuck in the ground by the boat.

"When's the reporter coming?" Leon asked Louie.

"Any minute. Hey, check out Hank," she said.

"*I've* got my executive jacket on, but he looks even better than me."

Hank blushed. One of the little girls shrieked. "Stop that," Todd yelled at the boy who had squirted her with his water pistol. "No guns. You get out of here if you're going to shoot that."

"Who says? You, tough guy?" the kid snarled.

"We're gonna have a water pistol shooting contest with a prize later this afternoon," Louie yelled.

"We are?" Todd asked her.

"Sure, why not," she said to him and to the kid, "Anyone who wants to enter has to sign up with me."

The kid looked at her as if she was crazy. His friend shoved him, grabbed the plastic gun, and ran off. The kid chased after his friend. Since they were heading out of his yard, Todd relaxed.

"What's the prize?" Leon asked Louie.

"For what?"

"For the water pistol shooting contest."

Louie grinned. "A kiss from me." Leon made a strangled sound and started up the hill to the house as if he had to throw up.

"Hey, serve up that soda so we can get out of here," an angry-faced kid shouted.

"Soon as the reporter gets here," Louie said.

"Reporter? What's he going to report? How many bottles of soda got drunk?"

"Listen," Louie called. "Listen, come in closer and listen to me. I want to tell you about our club."

"What club?"

One of the quiet little girls tugged at Louie's arm and Louie bent to hear what the child was saying. "Todd," Louie trumpeted. "Take this kid to the bathroom, will you? She's gotta go."

That got a laugh. Todd slunk through the catcalls and whistles, leading the little girl to the house. A chant began behind him and swelled to a roar. "Soda! We want our soda. Soda! We want our soda."

"My mommy's calling for us at twelve," the little girl told Todd. "Will the party be over by then?"

"I hope so," Todd mumbled.

The door of the half bathroom in the basement opened as Todd deposited the little girl in front of it. Leon walked out, and the little girl hurried in. Todd was eye to eye with his brother.

"That was the meanest thing you ever did to me, Leon," Todd burst out. "I never did anything to you. Why do you hate me so much?"

"I don't know what you're talking about," Leon said, pretending innocence as usual.

"You stole my island," Todd said with all his anguish sounding in his voice.

"I built you a clubhouse on your island and saved it from the river, you turkey," Leon said.

"But you stole the paper that says it's mine."

"What do you need the paper for if it's yours?"

"Proof. You said it yourself. I can't prove anything. Louie expects me to plant the flag, but I know you won't let me."

138

"Who says?"

The bathroom door opened. A soft small hand stole into Todd's. "I'm done," the little girl said.

"You'll let me claim the island?" Todd asked his brother.

"Try it and see," Leon said. He ran out of the basement and back down the hill. The child tugged at Todd's hand.

"Come on," she said.

Automatically, Todd walked down the hill with her. Did Leon mean it? Was it another trick? His voice had been neutral, but then Leon's voice was always neutral when he wanted to hide things.

"Got a new girlfriend, Todd?" B.J. asked. He and Joe had arrived and were standing by the table drinking a cup of the soda Louie had finally handed out. The crowd was quieter now.

"Okay, you guys, now listen to me," Louie was shouting hoarsely. She was so supercharged, Todd expected she'd give an electric shock to anyone standing next to her.

"What we're here for," Louie continued, "is to get some more members for our island club. See the clubhouse already there? You have to be a club member to use it. Now, how many of you here would like to be members of an exclusive island club with a clubhouse and all?"

"What's it for, this club?" a short, fat kid with a deep voice asked.

"For all kinds of things. We're going to have

meetings and parties and whatever else the members decide," Louie said.

"Who's in it so far?" the same boy asked.

"So far," Louie boomed, trying to cut through the noise of conversations. "So far there's me. I'm president." She bowed and smiled. "There's Todd over here. It's his island and he's going to plant the flag today. And there's Hank. Where's Hank hiding? Come out and say 'hi' to the folks, Hank. Don't be shy."

Kids were listening now and some laughed as Hank cringed back behind Leon.

"And there's Leon here," Louie said. "He practically built the clubhouse single-handed."

"I'm not in the club, though," Leon said.

"And Michael, he's a member for helping us if he wants to be." Louie hurried past Leon's disclaimer. "Now who else wants to join? Remember, we're not going to take too many. It's going to be an exclusive club like Todd here wants it."

"What do you have to do to join?" the fat kid asked.

"You just sign up and promise to do whatever I tell you and come to meetings and stuff like that."

"Who made you president?" the fat kid asked.

Louie stared at him. Then she glared at him. "I just *am*. I *am* the president," she said with passion.

"Presidents get elected," the fat kid said.

"Who'd want her for president!" the tall boy mocked and began to walk away followed by the

140

rest of the bicycle gang. They tossed their paper cups at the bushes as they swaggered back up the hill.

"Listen," Louie yelled. "Listen, one of the rules is you've got to accept the president. For one year. One year, I'm the president and after that you can elect somebody else."

A car horn honked. "That must be the reporter," Louie said. "Sit down everybody and listen."

"It's my mommy," the little girl whom Todd had chaperoned to the bathroom said. She and her friends rose, brushed off their bottoms, and trotted up the hill in a neat line.

The siren at the fire house screamed at twelve o'clock. The soda was gone. Kids began drifting off, following the trail set for them by early departures. They kept dropping their paper cups, popped balloons, a banana peel, and innumerable candy wrappers as they went.

Todd watched defeat sag from Louie's eyes to her mouth, which was still bleating appeals for everybody to listen. He felt too sorry for her to be relieved that the crowd was going.

"I wouldn't elect her for anything," he heard the lone girl left in the yard say.

"Louie'd be a good president," Todd said loudly. "She's full of ideas."

The girl gave him a scornful look and kept walking. In a minute only Louie, Hank, Leon, Michael, and Todd were left.

141

"What a mess," Leon said, looking around the lawn. Todd began picking up paper cups. Hank scurried around helping.

"I'll get a garbage bag from the house," Michael said.

"What happened?" Louie mourned. "What did I do wrong? I thought they were really going to go for it."

"Will the reporter still come?" Hank asked Todd anxiously.

"Who knows?" Todd answered. "Why do you want your picture in the paper, Hank? Nobody'll like you better for it."

"Yes, they will. The judge will." But he wouldn't explain any further when Todd asked him what he meant.

"They just didn't want me to be president," Louie was saying to nobody in particular. "I don't understand why nobody ever wants me. I'm such a great leader."

"Sure you are," Todd comforted her. "Anyway, you're still president of a club, an exclusive club, like you said, with me and Hank and you."

"Yeah," Louie sniffled. Then she tried to smile. "That's exclusive all right, isn't it? Just us three." A dimple showed in her cheek right below a sliding tear.

"And Michael and me can be honorary members," Leon offered charitably.

142

Todd looked at Leon to see if he was kidding, but Leon was gazing seriously at Louie. "Don't take it so hard," Leon said to her. "Politicians gotta learn to lose before they win."

Leon offering consolation to Louie? Todd was amazed.

By that time they'd fixed up the lawn, except for the trampled grass which was bent flat and muddied. Just as they were about to leave, a skinny man with a camera around his neck appeared in the driveway.

"Hey, here we are! You from the paper?" Louie sang out. She was shining with excitement again.

"You got it," the reporter said. "I'm Fox of the *Daily Gazette*. Who's the one who's claiming the island?"

"That's him," Louie said. "Todd Lewis." She spelled the name for the reporter. Todd held his breath, but Leon didn't say a word and Louie continued, "Todd's going to plant the flag. That's his island out there. . . . Want some soda? It's a little warm." Leon was still silent. Todd nearly burst. Was it really going to happen the way Louie said?

Fox said he wouldn't mind a cup, and they all waited while Louie poured him some. "Hot day," he said, wiping his mouth with the back of his hand and smiling at them. "Mind answering a few questions, Todd?"

"Uh uh," Todd said. He told Fox his age and

grade, but when Fox asked to see the official document that said the island was Todd's, he just stood there with his mouth hanging open.

"Did you leave it in the bathroom again?" Leon said suddenly. "That's where I saw it this morning. I'll go get it." And he did. He raced up to the house and came back with the much folded and now messy pink sheet. He handed it to the reporter.

"Good," Fox said after he had glanced at it. "Now, Todd, tell me what gave you the idea of laying claim to an island?"

"I wanted a place of my own," Todd said. It seemed as he said it that the notion came from a different time long past. "But now," he said in a daze of joy, "the clubhouse is for all of us, all the club members."

"You decided it was more fun to share?"

"No," Todd answered honestly. "It was just that I needed help. I couldn't have built the place up by myself, and —"

"And?"

"And it's more fun doing it together."

Fox nodded and asked, "So what are you planning to do on the island now that you've developed it?"

Nobody answered. Todd wondered how all this was going to come out in the paper.

"You going to camp out overnight on it?" Fox asked helpfully.

"Yeah," Todd said.

"Not me," Louie said. "I'm allergic to mosquitos."

"I'm just going to fish," Hank said. "My name is Hank Lewandowski. That's L-e-w-a-n-d-o-w-s-k-i. You gonna take a picture of us?"

"Yeah, in a minute," Fox said, grinning.

"And you boys, what do you want the island for?" Fox asked Leon and Michael.

"Nothing," Leon said and Michael shrugged.

"They're my brothers," Todd said. "If Leon and Michael hadn't helped, we wouldn't have anything, not even much of the sandbar. You see, Leon figured out how to shore up the end when the river started eating it. And then Leon showed us how to build the shack. He was kind of like our boss while we were building. Leon's a really good builder."

"Leon, how did you acquire such skills at your young age?" Fox asked.

"I don't know," Leon said modestly.

"He just does it naturally. He can take anything apart and put it together and make it work," Todd said. "He's always been that way."

"Okay," Fox said. "I guess that's enough. You kids stand together here and I'll take a picture of the group. Who's going to hold the flag? Todd, you're claiming the island, right?"

"Well, actually," Todd said, "I'm claiming it for us all. It belongs to all of us, everybody here." He felt instant relief, as if he'd taken one of those pain killers they advertise on television.

"Okay," Fox said. "Stand in closer. Todd, you hold the flag."

"Hey," Louie said. "Don't forget to put in that I'm president. Louanne LaVoy, president. You'll put that in, won't you?"

Hank stood up very straight in front of the group looking right at the camera. Louie grinned and made a V for victory sign. Leon and Michael stood beside Todd, who was holding his flag. He closed his eyes when the first picture was snapped, and turned his head to look at the island just as Fox took the second picture.

Todd insisted they all row out with him and be in the flag-planting ceremony. Fox sat in the rowboat, which was tethered to the lone tree. Todd poked the end of Louie's fishing pole in the ground near the clubhouse.

"Go ahead and say something, Todd," Louie told him.

"I claim this island in the name of . . . in the name of our club," Todd said. He wished he'd thought to make up a speech for the occasion. "And I name it, uh, Shoe Island, and I hope that we all get something good out of it and have fun here because — because we all put a lot into what's here, and it's our island. It belongs to all of us, Leon and Michael and Louie and Hank and me, and B.J. and Joe a little, too, I guess." He was surprised when they all applauded.

"That was a good speech," Leon said and slapped

him on the back knocking the air out of him. But Todd knew Leon meant well. It had been Leon's standard brotherly love tap.

Even getting the laser beam of Dad's silent anger shot at him for the squashed grass didn't take away Todd's delight that afternoon. When Louie called him after dinner, Todd told her he thought it had been a great flag-raising ceremony.

"Well, I guess it was okay," she said, "so long as Fox says it in the paper that I'm president. I can't wait for my father to see that."

Chapter 13

The picture of them planting the flag on the island appeared in the newspaper three days later. The shack and the flag showed clearly, and so did Hank, who faced the camera unsmiling. Louie stood next to him grinning, a head taller, her elbow on his shoulder. Leon and Michael were identifiable in profile and a headless body planting the flag was Todd. He breathed a sigh of relief when he saw it. Nobody could think he was showing off from that.

Everybody's name was spelled right, and the article noted that Louanne LaVoy, the only female involved, was the club's president. The reporter also gave Leon credit for his construction skills. Leon cut the write-up out immediately and took it to school with him. He didn't say anything, but Todd figured he must be pleased.

One boy in Todd's class even asked if it was too late to join the club. The boy had seen the picture in the paper that morning. He was a pretty nice kid too. Todd felt good. Everybody had gotten what they wanted, including him.

The mystery of Hank's remark about the judge was cleared up when Hank came over with his fishing rod one afternoon later in the week.

"I sent the newspaper picture to my mother, and she's going to send it to the family court judge so he'll see how good I'm being," Hank told Todd.

"The judge?" Todd asked.

"Yeah, the judge said my mother could have me back if I'm good for a whole year."

Todd was impressed with Hank's foresight, and he hoped the picture would help Hank's case.

As for the island, nobody went near it for weeks after the flag-raising. Louie had lost all interest in the place once the publicity was over. She had a new project for herself and Todd — collecting butterflies and other insects to make theirs the best collection anyone had ever turned in to their biology teacher. Louie did most of the collecting while Todd did most of the mounting and identifying. They made a good team. By the end of the first week and a half, they had more specimens than their closest competition, as near as Louie could assess.

One evening Todd was busy searching through books to identify some of the mounted insects when he found Leon looking over his shoulder.

"That's a pretty impressive collection, little brother," Leon said.

"Yeah, Louie's a great bug hunter," Todd agreed.

Leon laughed. "She's a character, all right." He didn't knock the boxes off the table or make Todd

149

lose his place in the encyclopedia of insects either.

"Ma," Todd asked the next afternoon when he and his mother were sitting on the grass at the ball field, swatting mosquitos and watching his brothers' Little League game. "How come Leon's being so nice to me lately?"

"Is he being nice?"

"Yeah. The only black and blue mark I got left is from when I tripped onto the school bus. Do you think he's maturing or something?"

She smiled. "Could be. Or it could be you who's changed, Todd. I know he was really pleased about that article in the paper. It was nice of you to give him credit for doing the building."

"How do you know I did?"

"He said as much to me. He also mentioned that he thinks you're learning how to be a friend. Something about how well you get along with Louie and Hank. I think you've impressed him."

Todd looked out at the field where Leon was winding up to pitch with his usual concentration. "Why should Leon care how I treat my friends?" He was asking the question of himself as much as of his mother, but she answered as if he had been talking to her.

"I don't know, but how you treat a friend says a lot about what kind of person you are, don't you think?"

"Yeah, I guess." Todd said. He wondered how it would be now that the island was developed. Was the summer coming up going to be spent with friends, or was he going to have to learn to be alone again? He hoped he wouldn't have to. Friends made life so much more interesting.

The next day Louie mentioned casually that her parents were sending her to a camp in Maine for most of the summer. Todd was busy absorbing that disappointment when Hank arrived at the rowboat where they were sitting.

"I came to tell you guys good-bye," Hank said. His smile was wide screen. "My mother's picking me up tonight. The judge decided to let me off early."

"But school's not even out yet." Louie said.

"Saint Agnes is done next week, and, anyway, nobody does any work the last days."

"Where?" Todd asked. "I mean, where's your real home?"

"Mechanicsville," Hank said. The three of them were silent. Mechanicsville was close enough so they'd heard of it, but too far away for visiting.

"Think you'll ever come back?" Todd asked.

"I don't know," Hank said. His smile slipped away.

"We're going to miss you," Louie said. "Listen, you can still be a club member even if you can't attend meetings."

"Thanks," Hank said. He stuck out his hand. First Todd and then Louie shook it. Then Hank started walking back up the hill.

When he turned to wave, Louie said, "Don't forget to write."

"I won't," Hank said.

Todd wondered if Hank meant he wouldn't forget or he wouldn't write. In any case, it looked as if he wasn't going to have any friends to spend the summer with after all.

One warm weekend late in June, Leon said to Todd, "You ever going to use that camp we built?"

"Yeah," Todd said. "I'm gonna take a flashlight and my sky chart over there some night and learn to spot constellations."

"How about going tonight? You and me and Michael could camp out together."

"Hey, that'd be nice," Todd said, and he didn't even wonder if Leon planned to drown him or suffocate him in his sleeping bag.

They loaded their gear into the rowboat after dinner when it was still light out. Dad chased down the hill after them before they cast off from shore, but it was just to give them a can of bug juice to fend off the mosquitos. "They're hungry tonight," Dad said and grinned.

The island floated in the hush of evening. Silver arcs lifted from the river as fish jumped. Birds trilled their nightly farewells. The water passed by so slowly that Todd couldn't even hear it lap against the pebble-strewn shore. With his back to their house, Todd could have been a thousand miles from home. He had a sense of belonging to the earth and keeping time with its rhythms.

Leon sent Michael and Todd back to shore to gather firewood in the mirrored light of evening. When enough stars showed, Todd deserted the anemic fire, which kept trying to go out. He took his flashlight and star chart to the breakwater where Michael and Leon soon joined him.

"Next time we got to get a pile of firewood ready and leave it on the island beforehand," Leon said.

"How come it looks like there's more stars here than there are from the house?" Michael asked.

"Because it's darker here," Leon said. "Right, little brother?"

"Right," Todd said. He flashed his light on the chart. Leon studied it too. A night hum of buzzing, chirruping insects surrounded them. Leon pointed up toward Polaris. Todd found the W of Cassiopeia. Orion was easy to spot because of the three stars close together in a row across his belt and the four outside stars boxing that.

Todd thought he saw Cepheus but Leon said no. They argued until Michael said, "Hey, you guys, what's the difference? Let it go, huh?"

Todd stopped talking immediately. He thought he was right, but Michael was righter. Leon stopped too. "Why don't you tell us a story, Michael?" Leon said.

Michael began telling them one of the rambling tales that he seemed to invent as he went along, about a man who lived all alone on an island and killed any boatman who came near his shore because he'd gone crazy from a terrible event that had wiped out his family. Then Leon told the old story of the ghostly hitchhiker. By then it was hard to tell whether they were shivering from fear or from the cold. They unrolled their sleeping bags, which just fitted side by side in the shack.

Todd zipped himself into his bag and looked out the open doorway, far out into the dark, mysterious vastness of space. Leon and Michael settled down on either side of him. Todd felt safe cocooned in his sleeping bag between his brothers.

"You know, this is really fun," he said.

"Yeah," Leon said. "Camping out is fun."

"No, I mean, being together with you guys, that's fun."

"Aw, go to sleep, little brother," Leon said.

But Todd was too happy to sleep. In his whole life he couldn't remember a night as wonderful as this one had been. Somehow he had gained a treasure even better than an island of his own.